Sometimes it's hard to tell if Wren and Kevin have two sets of parents or no parents at all. On weekend trips to the state mental hospital they visit their father, who has slipped silently and painfully into his own world. Their mother, too, has a life apart from her children—one of fashion, big cities, and an independence neither Wren nor Kevin can accept. At times it feels as though a whole generation has been lost, and Wren and Kevin are caught somewhere in between. . . .

Their grandmother, Bliss, is always at the center dispelling the myths of craziness which lurk in the background of the Jackson family. But is Bliss enough to see her grandchildren through the frightening crash with reality that threatens Wren's dreams and Kevin's own survival?

Throughout it all, there is music—for Bliss to sing, for Wren to play, and for Kevin to turn to—notes to carry them to another life. Once again, Sue Ellen Bridgers reaches into our hearts with a story of loss and betrayal, and of a truly special love between a brother and sister. Like a well-loved and beautiful song, *Notes for Another Life* will linger long after the last page . . . a family chronicle for all ages to be read again and again.

Also by Sue Ellen Bridgers

HOME BEFORE DARK

ALL TOGETHER NOW

NOTES
for another
LIFE

A Novel by
SUE ELLEN BRIDGERS

Alfred A. Knopf ✺ *New York*

For Sandra and Abbott
who have shared with me a common life
And for Lynn and for Ben
who have joined us in it

THIS IS A BORZOI BOOK
PUBLISHED BY ALFRED A. KNOPF, INC.

Library of Congress Cataloging in Publication Data
Bridgers, Sue Ellen. Notes for another life.
Summary: Tom Jackson's mental illness is difficult for his entire family,
but particularly so for his sixteen-year-old son Kevin
who wonders if he has the same affliction.
[1. Mental illness—Fiction. 2. Suicide—Fiction] I. Title.
PZ7.B7615No 1981 [Fic] 81–1673
ISBN 0–394–84889–6   AACR2
ISBN 0–394–94889–0 (lib. bdg.)

Notes *for* Another Life

Chapter 1

On their way to the hospital, Wren and her grandmother would start out singing. Wren sat close to the window, pressed hard against her confinement, her eyes searching for signs of spring across the flat open space of fields. Looking out, she could force her mind away from her mission until a border of dark woods abruptly limited the morning sky and closed her in. Then she would have to remember where she was going and why.

Beside her, her grandmother Bliss wore her spring coat, rose-colored on its surface but worn at the edges to a dusty brown so that her face and hands seemed to float out of the fading hues of the old Cadillac's upholstery. Bliss' hands were tight on the wheel when they began, as if she must force the car on its familiar trek. But singing, she relaxed a little. Her hands softened on the leather casing, and she thrust her head out of the collar of her coat, craning upward to find the notes. After a few minutes she hardly noticed the road at all. She knew the road.

She knew the songs, too, for they were out of her memory—"As Time Goes By," "When the Red-Red Robin Comes Bob-Bob-Bobbing Along," "Whispering." She had taught them to her grandchild, and so, after the first couple of notes, Wren closed her eyes to find the alto.

There were years of harmony between them. They knew the pitch, the range of their duets, as well as they knew any other habits after six years together. It was that long since Wren had come to live with her grandparents. She could remember how, at seven, she had quavered on the high notes that came to Bliss with such ease. Now, at thirteen, Wren had discovered the same ease in her own voice. She understood the music, seeing in her head the notes her grandmother had taught her, but she also knew what the singing was for. She felt it pull them together, bringing comfort and courage against the panic that accompanied every visit to her father. What if he were different? they would wonder, leaning slightly toward each other as they sang. But even worse, what if he were the same?

"What about 'I'll Be Seeing You'?" Bliss asked and started in before Wren could nod her approval.

Wren never suggested new songs, although once she had hummed a Barry Manilow tune on the edge of her breath, loud enough for Bliss to hear.

"Nice enough," Bliss said after a few bars, "but can it equal this?" And was off into "Can't Help Loving Dat Man of Mine."

So they sang down thirty miles of highway until the car turned up the drive to the state mental hospital. There between the shadows of oaks lining the road, a knife edge of dread slid against Wren's chest so that her lips whispered the words for a few drifting bars, and she was quiet. They stopped their singing then as if the melodies, so old and rich with feeling, had to stay trapped in the fading luxury of Bliss' old car. They had never heard music in this place, and so they sat in the parking lot waiting for the sounds in their heads to die away, fold up like the worn paper leaves of sheet music in the walnut cabinet at home.

Wren heard the silence and attuned herself to it. It was the silence of her father's room, an absence of any discernible feeling. The room was always empty to her, no matter how many people came into it: the doctor who held Bliss' hand while he talked as if he needed to touch someone's understanding of his failure to revive this patient; the orderly who pushed the straw between her father's lips and commanded him to suck; the roommate who was always asking for a light because matches were forbidden. Even her grandmother seemed distant and unnatural in that hospital room, as though, out of desperation, she had consented to play an impossible role for an hour.

"Are you ready?" Wren asked, watching her grandmother's profile, the fine wrinkles, the soft swirls of graying hair, the parted lips slowly setting themselves with the determined look of a woman who had and would endure.

What was she thinking? Wren wondered. Perhaps her mind turned toward some long-ago memory of her son Tom, how he'd once been such a live wire he'd kept the neighborhood in stitches with his antics, how he'd been the most popular boy in his class, the family clown.

"Grandmother, are you ready?"

"Of course I am," Bliss said.

But neither of them ever was.

They stopped at the drugstore on their way home. Kevin was behind the lunch counter, wearing a white paper hat and a bib apron tied around his waist. He looked haggard and older than his sixteen years although there was an unfinished look about him, too, as if his features had not quite settled into a reliable face. He didn't seem to know how to pull himself together yet.

"I overslept," he said sheepishly to his grandmother, who sat down at the counter and slipped her purse onto the shelf below.

"Ham on rye," Bliss said. "How about you, Wren?"

Wren gave the stool next to her a spin. "The same. And a Coke, Kevin. A big one."

"I really intended to go with you today," Kevin said. "Honest."

"I know you did," Bliss said. "It's all right."

Wren and Bliss watched his back, saw relief creep into the set of his shoulders. They knew he couldn't bring himself to see his father anymore.

"I think he's better, Kevin," Wren said and then took a deep breath, deciding to go on. It was easier to tell him here in public than at home where he'd feel obligated to react. "He was lying on his back instead of toward the wall. And the doctor said they may start the treatments in a few days. You know they always bring him around."

"For a while." Kevin was looking at her through the mirror. She looked so confident. He wished he were thirteen again and had hope.

"What about lunch?" Bliss asked. "I have things to do this afternoon."

Kevin busied himself with the sandwiches, but he kept

6

glancing into the mirror watching Wren as he sliced the meat. She was getting pretty. All of a sudden her face was thinning out, eyes taking on a luminous quality, skin coming alive after winter's pallor.

"Where's Granddaddy?" she wanted to know.

"In the back." Kevin was holding a paper cup under the Coke fountain. "We got a big shipment of drugs this morning. I was going to help him but then Ginny called in sick and that left me out here by myself. On top of that, Mother called." He turned to them with sandwiches— triangles of rye—chips, strips of dill pickle on the side. "She's coming next week for a couple of days. She has something to tell us, something about her job, I guess. I didn't say anything about Dad being back in the hospital. I mean, what difference would it make?"

"You did the right thing, Kevin," Bliss said, looking straight at him. The sight of her lunch sickened her now. She was thinking she'd have to air her son's room, the room he and Karen had shared years ago when they were first married and had come home from college with no prospects but expecting everything to take care of itself.

Bliss had been the one to take care. She'd fed them, clothed them, put a roof over their heads that first year when Tom was struggling to get started in the insurance business and Karen was expecting Kevin.

All that time they were fixing up a house on the next block, and so when the baby was born, they went home to the bright little house, so cleverly decorated that the neighbors were astonished that such fabric, paints, and rugs were to be found for any price, much less on a shoestring. Karen had been unwilling to take the run-of-the-mill product that was available locally and that everybody else had. So her house reflected eclectic taste and also, Bliss had felt even then, a vision of herself apart from the life romantic love had offered her.

"Grandmother," Wren was saying. "Maybe Mother's coming home to stay."

"Don't count on it," Kevin said. He poured coffee into Bliss' cup.

"But maybe when she knows Daddy's sick again, when she sees him . . ." Wren paused, hearing the futility of her own words. "When she sees us," she blurted out, unable to stop herself.

There, it was said. The three of them stopped, trapped by the unspoken answer that no one had the courage to speak, and let the words drift into the acrid smell of the old drugstore, lost to them like smoke.

"Don't think that, Wren," Kevin said softly. He rested his hand on her shoulder. She seemed frail to him, and he could feel a narrow tremble down her back, a sigh of longing to have her parents again. "Don't ever think that."

Chapter 2

Wren was singing in the Baptist Church choir. They had finished the Call to Worship and were sitting now, their crimson robes billowing around them in the auditorium seats of the choir loft. The choir was behind the pulpit, and so they could look out at the bowed heads of the congregation or else at the minister's back.

Mr. Kensley in his black robe, a new and controversial addition to the growing ritual of the church. Mr. Kensley was new, young, and untrustworthy, having brought with him from the seminary the latest in liturgics—responsive readings printed in the bulletin, an occasional recitation of the Articles of Faith, a black robe. He would have them on their knees yet, members worried among themselves, preparing their arguments in advance for the presentation of complaints they expected to make in the event some future straw finally broke the camel's back.

The congregation shuffled irreverently while Mr. Kensley lowered his towhead, as white as sunlight through the clear spaces of glass above the colored windows, and prayed for criminals and dope addicts. "And for the mentally ill," he added softly, which brought Wren's attention around. She looked up toward the bowed heads to see Kevin looking straight ahead as if he weren't hearing a word. He wasn't even pretending.

She tried to catch his eye. Look at me, she willed him. See me. And he did. She smiled a little, seeing a glimmer of recognition crossing his empty face.

They were thinking of their father, a fleeting image that they let pass quickly between them. Then Kevin's face broadened and Wren knew he was now remembering Aunt Carolina Jackson, their long-dead relative who may not exactly have been mentally ill but who was nevertheless a nuisance, for she believed she could sing and could not. She did sing, however, because there was no stopping her. Bliss told them that once, years ago, Carolina stood up in this very choir loft, while the minister caught his breath between sentences in his exegesis of the fifth beatitude, and sang "Don't Sit Under the Apple Tree" completely off key but without missing a beat. Bliss told them such a story with lightness in her voice as if she could sprinkle the past craziness of the Jackson family on them ever so gently, like confetti to be brushed away. They needed to know their heritage simply because everybody else in town knew it, not because it mattered any.

Kevin looked away from his sister's place in the choir loft. She seemed so far away, separated from him by nodding heads, prim shoulders, the minister's resonant tone; and so he glanced at Melanie Washburn, who sat beside him on the back row and whose hand he held under the folded jacket on her lap.

He had been dating Melanie ever since he'd gotten his

driver's license six months ago and his grandparents had given him the drugstore station wagon on weekends. The wagon was compact and orange and had *Jackson Pharmacy Quality Service since 1935* and the phone number on its sides, but it was better than no wheels at all.

Now he held Melanie's fingers lightly, as if he must be prepared to pull away quickly. This tentative touching was something he'd had to learn. Once he had held on to his parents, pulling at their fingers, forcing himself into their arms, burying his nose in his mother's scent, his head weighting his father's shoulder. But they had wrenched away, both of them, no matter how he tried to hold on, and so he had learned to touch carelessly, exposing no need of his own with his hands. He was always ready to let go.

Still his fingers crept up Melanie's wrist, touching the smooth flesh, the tiny bones. He loved her wrist, the expensive gold watch she'd gotten for her birthday, the fine gold chain he'd given her that was always caught in it—his small gift linked to the elegant one her parents had offered. She never took the chain off.

His fingers slid off her wrist, back down to the palm she held open beneath the coat. Her head was bowed, eyes closed, as if she didn't feel his touch. It was just as well, Kevin thought, and wished he could deny what he felt about her.

Perhaps he had learned not to hold on tightly, but he knew something held him now, a feeling for Melanie, a constant longing to hold her hand like this, to have her in the car beside him when they cruised Hardee's, to sip the same Coke at the movies, order a pizza from Barney's and share it parked along the river while the town brightened the sky with street lights and car lights as if dawn were continually breaking across the river.

Wren saw Kevin shifting his attention to Melanie Washburn who was his girl friend, she supposed, since Kevin wasn't dating anyone else. After all these months, she was still surprised that Melanie and Kevin had been attracted to each other at all. Melanie belonged to the right clubs, all of which Kevin made a point of avoiding. She made good grades and had a natural easy exuberance, while Kevin was quiet, sometimes even humorless, as if light-heartedness carried an exorbitant price.

She didn't know what Kevin and Melanie did together, although she knew they must park along the river because everybody who had a car did. She didn't want to know what happened between them, although she had been the one to discover a beer can wedged under the seat and had been in the hall between the bathroom and bedroom once when Kevin came up the stairs at midnight, his shirttail flapping beneath his jacket and his lips puffy. Wren didn't say anything about his looks or about the beer can, which she put in the trash at the store where it would go unnoticed by her grandparents.

She didn't know exactly what protection she could provide Kevin, but she offered it nonetheless. Protection against their grandparents' silent concern, against their mother thinking them less than perfect, against upsetting their father's unsteady progress with yet another situation he was incapable of handling. She and Kevin must never be a bother. It was an unspoken commitment between them, bonded by the regret their father's illness had brought them and the untraversable distance their mother kept.

Beside Wren, her best friend, Jolene, was flipping the
pages of the hymnal soundlessly, waiting for the prayer to
end. Then they would get up and sing because it was Young
People's Sunday and Jolene and Wren had been practicing
"Savior Like a Shepherd Lead Us" every Wednesday night
for two months, so often that Wren no longer even knew the
tune, which Jolene sang, but heard instead the alto, which
had become for her as familiar as the melody had once been.

Jolene had lost her place. They could hear Mr. Kensley
winding up his prayer, and she fingered the hymnal
frantically, searching for the slip of paper that marked the
duet. Wren opened the book on her lap calmly, her finger
having securely kept the page all though the interminable
prayer, and showed Jolene the number. Jolene snickered
nervously. She was always panicky and on the verge of
upset.

"I'm scared," she mouthed.

"Sh-h-h," Wren said softly.

They heard the Amen, then the brief silence while the
minister settled himself in his chair in front of them, and
finally the rising chord of the organ. They stood up
together, matching brown curly heads and pleated robes,
identical pale pink lip gloss and cheek blush, tiny pearls
piercing their ears.

Jolene looked at the book frantically, seeking out the
familiar pattern of words and notes. But Wren looked up
and out to see first her brother's embarrassed glance in the
direction of his sweetheart; then at her grandparents, Bliss
and Bill Jackson, center pew on the left aisle, where they
had sat for years. They were smiling up at her, Bliss' gloved
fingers curled beneath her chin, Bill's arm across the back of

the pew, sheltering her. For a fleeting moment before her first note appeared in her head like a reward she had earned, Wren thought to herself how almost everything she loved was in this room; and when the note came, it was as sure and confident as her grandmother's smile.

Jolene, relieved to have the song over, nudged Wren in the ribs and lowered her head to exchange a silly, euphoric grin. Now Jolene's mother, who sat down the pew from Wren's grandparents, could breathe. She was fanning herself steadily with the bulletin as if a flash of heat had overcome her while her daughter stood, eyes toward heaven, and sang slightly flat but so sweetly.

At least it was done, Wren thought, and not badly, although she knew it could have been improved. She took music much more seriously than Jolene, who sang because she liked being the center of attention rather than for any love of music. For Wren it was different. Ever since she was small and had balanced on Bliss' lap, gravely curving her tiny fingers to the piano keys, she had known that music would always be essential to her life. She had been drawn to it, just as some people had a natural inclination for the rhythm of words and other people, the language of motion. She had understood so much about music instinctively that working for perfection in it seemed both natural and compelling.

Wren felt another quick nudge from Jolene, and so she turned her attention toward the back of the boy at the lectern. Sam Holland was preaching. Jolene giggled, her head still tucked to her chest. Sam Holland! Who would have guessed!

They didn't see Sam anymore since he was in the ninth grade, a high school freshman. He belonged to a different church, too, one of the three in town combining efforts for this special service, and so he seemed incongruous behind their lectern in his khaki-colored suit, his hair carefully feathered and brushed but curling slightly at the ends and around the temples because he was getting hot up there, on display as he was.

His notes seemed to be slipping away from him, curling up under his anxious fingers as he tried to organize them. He held his elbows tight to his body, but one knee was bent slightly, leaning his weight toward the support of the heavy, scrolled lectern.

Wren had never liked Sam Holland, although she'd never really known him. From her distance, he'd always seemed too perfect to her, so good at everything that making a show came natural to him and he did it effortlessly, as if being a star was what he expected. One year behind him all through grade school, Wren had seen him play football, basketball, baseball—to every season there was an organized sport— had seen him in the corridors and the lunchroom and at the eighth-grade dances last year, all of which she attended with Jimmy down the street, who would never ask anyone but her. She was the only girl Jimmy really knew, for he had taken the same route home from school year after year, had played basketball in front of her garage and sat in their kitchen having a soft drink because Bliss wanted young people in the house, companions for the deserted children she harbored.

At the dances, Wren had seen Sam Holland with a girl, always a different one and always pretty. She had seen him dance and had known that dancing came as naturally to him as everything else did. He hadn't struggled in front of a mirror like Jimmy had. Jimmy danced as if his knees were permanently locked, but there was something dear about his determination to get it right, to please her. Sam Holland had always seemed intent on pleasing himself.

And here he was delivering the sermon, an assortment of what sounded like newspaper headlines about the impending crises of the world and their obligation to do something about them.

But what? Wren wondered, beginning to listen more carefully. What could she, or even Sam Holland, do about anything? Weren't they helpless against inflation, the spread of Communism, hunger, cancer, mental illness? Didn't she, saddled with the obligation to avoid conflict with her grandparents, let alone her father, have responsibilities enough?

His voice irritated her. He was sounding so confident now, having conquered those first squirming doubts that accompanied momentary stage fright. He had practiced his message as many times as she and Jolene had been through their song. He knew it by heart, had considered every sentence structure, every verb agreement. But did he know what he was asking of her, that she become superwoman to his superman? He who had no problems more obvious than an occasional zit camouflaged under Clearasil, who could score the winning basket, write the prize-winning essay, dance like every joint in his body contained a liquid rhythm?

His papers fluttered slightly, one having stuck to his sweaty palm. He faltered a little, misreading a sentence he had probably seen a hundred times with his eyes shut. It was about service to the community, how the community encompassed the world, how the world under the thrust of science and technology grew smaller daily, more attainable but more fraught with risks and responsibilities.

He stumbled again, this time ever so slightly, a muffled word caught on a shudder of breath that from the looks of the congregation had gone unnoticed. But Wren heard.

He is not so sure, she thought suddenly, staring at the broadening shoulders, the tight elbows, the shiny heels of his carefully polished shoes. All this promise of the future, all this obligation to make something of oneself, to contribute, weighed heavily on him, pushed him deeper into the wooden arms of the lectern.

He was finished, the last words strong and piercing, but for Wren they sounded somehow desperate, betrayed fading confidence.

Who is this person? she wondered, standing for the final hymn. She pressed her hymnal against her chest as he turned toward her. He looked her straight in the face for a split second before he opened his own hymnal, his back to her again.

Her knees trembled. So did his. She could see him calming himself, taking slow breaths he'd learned to take in basketball games when the heat was on. He held the hymnal out from his body, one hand spread behind it, the other pressing the page flat. She pushed her own hymnal away from her chest and settled it on her hand just as he had. They began to sing.

Beside her, Jolene stretched her voice up and over the congregation, still basking in the success of their performance. But Wren saw the words in a blur, her eyes focusing two places at once so that they wavered over the alto line and finally settled on the profile of Sam Holland, who had turned slightly in her direction as if he wanted to look behind and discover her searching, feverish face.

Who are you? she asked silently, hearing the bellowing chorus around her. Why are you different today?

But even then, studying the suddenly beautiful, tense profile that fell into her vision, she knew that who she really questioned was herself. For at that moment, so splendid that it spun about her head like an invisible halo, she felt completely, irrevocably, new.

Chapter 3

Karen came on Tuesday. Wren saw her car, an old gray Peugeot, in the driveway when she turned the corner after school. There it was beside Bliss' ancient Cadillac, both of them looking shabby but nevertheless evoking an ageless quality of elegance as if they belonged to a more prosperous time, an older, more substantial middle class.

Bliss always said you could tell the old middle class from the new one by their porch furniture: the old had wicker, the new had folding aluminum. Naturally, the Jacksons had a wicker sun porch, a loveseat and two chairs painted glossy white, a bent willow rocker Bill Jackson sat in, and a tall porch table on which Bliss cultivated a gigantic fern, its tendrils cascading to the crushed tile floor.

The house was red brick with white trim, black shutters with curved latches, and a charcoal roof that capped the two stories solidly. There was a bay window with velvet window seat and antique satin draperies, the baby grand piano visible through the small panes when the sun was right. It was a house that said conscientious people lived there amid the pruned and dusted shrubs and flowering fruit trees.

Wren loved it, her home for six years, although its

familiarity had begun long before that, as far back as her baby life when she had had a crib in the spare room and her father's old highchair in the kitchen. Now everything she owned was there, protected within those sturdy walls. Books and records, old toys and stuffed animals, artwork from the first grade, abandoned doll carriage and miniature kitchen stove. Her whole life was in that house.

And now her mother was there, too. Wren shifted her backpack off her shoulders and held it in front of her. Inside the pack, in a little leather pouch, she had a folding comb, lip gloss, and a tiny art nouveau mirror Jolene had given her for Christmas. She could get ready right here on the street, stop under the elm tree in Mrs. Baker's sideyard and roll her fringe of winged bangs backward against her hand, brighten her lips, pinch her cheeks. But it seemed so unsatisfactory to do that, for she knew fixing her face wasn't the kind of preparation this event required.

I mustn't cry, she thought, parking herself momentarily under Mrs. Baker's elm and hugging her backpack. I always cry when I see her, but today I won't. I promise I won't. She took a deep breath and tightened her arms around the backpack.

I will not cry, she said to herself. I will not. But halfway down the street, she felt the tears come.

Karen was in the kitchen with Bliss. She sat at the kitchen table in front of the large windows that looked out on the spring blooms in Bliss' garden. The blurred colored light off the red and yellow tulips behind her seemed to brighten the picture she made, illumined the auburn hair that framed her profile—smooth, silken hair, as manageable as everything else about her.

Chapter Three

Her hand rested beside Bliss' china teapot, the fingers spread as if she were controlling a desire she had to jump up and fly away, leaving them again after a cup of tea and the meager warmth of their home fire. She was wearing a new color, something between blue and green, and a fuchsia blouse, startlingly rich. It resembled the outfits she put on mannequins in Atlanta and were not the kind of clothes a mother wore.

"You're home," Karen said, seeing Wren in the doorway, her backpack still hugged to her chest, tears welling and ready to spill.

"You, too." Wren dropped the pack.

Karen didn't get up but turned her chair and body slightly away from the table so that there was room for her daughter to come to her, arms around each other, heads touching, silk against the natural friz Wren battled with. Wren slid into her lap, curled up like a baby, feeling the smooth fabric of her mother's clothes, the narrow body, chest almost as flat as her own. Karen was always on a diet, always eating health food, fish and fowl, icy raw vegetables, sipping herb tea, on the run. It was not, she reminded them, what children liked, craving as they did milk shakes, hamburgers and fries, pizza, layer cake.

"How's my sweetheart?" Karen said into Wren's cheek, nuzzling her. "She's grown two inches at least," to Bliss over Wren's head.

"And five pounds. She's perfect for her age," Bliss replied. She was rinsing spring lettuce under the vegetable sprayer at the sink. The ruffled leaves glistened in her hands.

"You're staying tonight, aren't you?" Wren asked.

"Yes." Karen kissed her daughter's head. "Gee, your hair smells terrific," she said. And they all laughed.

"Is Kevin home yet?" Wren asked, popping out of her mother's arms. Lingering there had embarrassed her a little, as if she were showing more need than was reasonable. She didn't want to make demands, knowing how uncomfortably they could be met. It was better to let her mother be.

"He stopped by the store," Bliss said. "Your granddaddy called to see if Karen had arrived, and so he's sending Kevin along." She swished the lettuce in a wire basket, splattering her arms and apron with water.

Wren was beside her, getting milk from the refrigerator. They looked at each other for a second, acknowledging their shared sense of apprehension about Kevin. He was so moody lately, going straight from school to the drugstore or to tennis practice, then home for dinner, a few minutes on the phone with Melanie and then into his room where he crawled into his rumpled bed, sometimes still wearing his clothes, and fell into an exhausted, fitful sleep. Only Melanie seemed to bring him out, punctuated his solemnity with her laughter, pulling him along with her unflagging urging to shape up and enjoy himself.

She's good for him, Bliss thought, but how long can it last?

"He'll be here soon, I'm sure," she said aloud. "When you finish your snack, you can take your mother's things up."

Wren nodded, knowing her grandmother wanted to see Kevin alone, to make sure he was all right before Karen saw him. She would take a minute to prepare him, but not just brush his hair across his forehead with her fingers or adjust his collar as if he were about to be photographed. She would do more than that, hugging him to her although he shunned embraces. She would be reminding him that she was always there, this house was always his. No matter what Karen had come to tell them, it wouldn't have to make a difference in his life.

But both of them knew it did. What Karen was doing out of their sight in Atlanta always mattered. Her absence counted; it was a minus, a subtraction from the sum of their lives because it meant, no matter how they struggled to deny it, that she didn't need them enough, want them enough, love them enough.

Upstairs in the room she had long ago shared with Tom Jackson, Karen took off her jacket and flung it on the end of the bed, then dropped onto the bed herself, her head against the pillow sham. Returning to this room always caught her off guard no matter how she tried to prepare herself, and so she closed her eyes to enhance the transition back into this life she'd left years ago. It had never been easy to come back, and this time was no different. Regrets nagged at her. Perhaps she could have been more patient, given Tom more time, and yet she didn't think either her staying or her going could have mattered much to him. When she left for good, nothing had mattered to Tom but himself.

But the children. She had left her children, too, although she had felt herself separate from them long before she left. She had coped with Tom's illness by focusing on her job with a local department store, fitting contorted plaster bodies into clothes with hidden seams, fabric bunched and pinned under arms and at waists. She had fashioned images behind glass, arranged wire bodies, fastened sunglasses to unseeing eyes. She had avoided both her children and Tom while living in the same house with them. She couldn't listen to the doctor's skeptical prognosis, his experimental procedure for cure. There was no cure, and so Bliss was more and more in charge of the appointments, the urgings to eat and look, the laborious prayers when one is not quite sure what to pray for. Relief? Release? Or should it be for courage, patience, long-suffering acceptance?

Release was what she wanted, and so she took a job designing windows for a gigantic store six hours away in Atlanta. She would find a place big enough for Kevin and Wren to live with her after a year, as soon as she'd made the necessary job adjustments and accumulated a couple of raises. She had come back often at first, and yet each time the children had changed, grown gangly, toothy, hesitant in their affection. They seemed to belong to her less and less, to need her less and less, and so she never arranged for them to come live with her.

Now she opened her eyes to look at Wren, who had put the suitcase down carefully and was opening the blinds. Afternoon light slanted onto the floor at her feet.

"Come. Sit here beside me," Karen said, patting the bed next to her.

Wren stretched out on her father's side. Her legs were as long as her mother's, and the sight of them—her mother in sheer stockings, expensive heels, Wren in old Levi's and Nikes—reminded her so acutely of the distance between them that Wren squeezed her eyes shut, refusing to see.

"What is it, Wren?" Karen asked, seeing her daughter's grimace. She took Wren's hand.

Wren could only think that this touching which reached across four months didn't seem hard to her mother. It had been Christmas when Karen had last appeared, Peugeot as brightly burdened as any sleigh as it brought her city riches. She had been tearful at midnight in the candlelit church while her daughter bent toward the guitar balanced on her knee, to sing "Silent Night," her hair glistening darkly like a burnished halo. She had sampled their eggnog, their fruitcake, embraced their gifts, wrapped herself in their month's preparation because her coming was a happening as eventful to them as the arrival their faith celebrated.

And then she was gone. On Christmas afternoon the Peugeot, sleek and light against the gray sky, sped out of the snow-swept driveway and turned the corner, red lights hanging in the snowy sky, the turn signal winking at them.

Wren let the memory pass and opened her eyes. "Grandmother told you about Daddy, didn't she?"

"Yes, but she didn't have to. He's obviously not here." Karen sighed and rubbed her fingers across the top of Wren's hand. "How long this time?"

"It started in January. But he's been in the hospital just three weeks. They're giving him a new kind of medicine."

"They've always been giving him a new kind of medicine. For eight years now, he's been an experiment."

"But he's a little better." Wren wished she could pull her hand away. She wanted to and yet her mother's touch seemed so essential to her, like a gift one couldn't afford to refuse. "Anyway, they're talking about shock treatments. That's helped him before. Remember?"

"Yes, I remember." Karen let go her hand.

Wren felt such a loss that she wrapped her arms quickly across her chest, holding herself.

"I know exactly how he gets better, almost like himself but not quite. Always holding some part of himself back like a hurt he's protecting." Karen's voice was edged with bitterness. "I know how it lasts a year, sometimes even two. And then one day he is here on this bed and he says he feels nauseated, he has the flu, and so he stays in bed. Day after day he sleeps, eating less and less, talking less and less, until one morning he doesn't eat at all, doesn't talk at all, doesn't even sleep anymore. Just lies here staring." Karen stopped and reached out for Wren. "I'm sorry, sweetheart. I shouldn't be talking like this."

"It's nothing she doesn't know," Kevin said from the doorway.

"Kevin!" Karen held out her arms to him.

He came slowly, as if he would keep her there, arms outstretched to him for as long as he could. Why doesn't she ever come to me? he wondered. She calls, she drives here every few months, but she never touches first, never takes steps.

He was in her arms, cuddled to her breasts, his face at the pulse in her throat. He could feel her taking him in, absorbing him in her smell, her soft hands in his hair, her breath on his face. He stayed there, kneeling beside the bed with her arms around him for as long as he dared, until he felt a sob grumbling in his gut, some pitiful savage cry of longing to be there forever. He pulled away then, knowing he was risking too much. He knew his mother could see it if she were willing to look at how his mouth trembled and his chest heaved to push down the sob. But she didn't look.

Chapter Three

Only Wren saw. She got up quickly and went to the window, turning away from them because she knew what was coming. Kevin would not wait for Karen's news.

"What did you come to tell us?" he asked. He was standing over his mother, a coarse, ill-fitting shield of bravery between them.

"I'm moving to Chicago. It's a promotion, a really big one. We have four stores there, three in shopping centers and one downtown. I'll be in charge of all the windows, be responsible for the concepts—" She paused, looking from one of her children to the other.

Wren's back was to her, shoulders slumped forward. Kevin faced her, fists clinching at his sides, face grim and unresponsive, a sullen mannequin. It was hard for Karen to believe that he'd once been such an eager child, so ready to explore, to be held, to return affection. He had been intense, too, sensitive to moods, the nuances of feeling. Now that was closed off, like a door shut against her.

"It wouldn't work for you to come with me. I'll be living in an apartment in a big city, working long hours. You'd have to fend for yourselves, start in new schools, make new friends. There's no point in your having to do all that when you have your grandparents right here, this lovely house to live in, your friends, your father."

Karen paused, waiting for a response that didn't come. The silence seemed to ache around them, an old wound reopened. She stood up, panicked a little by their refusal to make it easier for her. What could she say to make them understand that she truly loved them but that at the same time her decision to go to Chicago could not be affected by what she felt for them. She had never intended for their lives to end up like this, separate, the problems and pleasures of day-to-day existence forever avoided. It had been a sin of omission, not of intent, that had kept them apart. And now, almost grown as they were, couldn't they see that she had two parallel lives, one as important to her as the other?

"If you weren't with your family, if you weren't in the town where you were born, if you weren't happy here, I'd take you. You know that. We would make arrangements if it were necessary. But it isn't," she said. She knew her news was settling in to them like a recurrent injury, reminding them of her first tearful departure. But what could she do? Life was more complicated than they knew. There were decisions made on a moment's notice, with other considerations left until the quiet of night when her mind boggled on them, harassing her with the possibility of negligence. She rushed on. "I don't suppose you even want to come, anyway. You're all right. I can see that. You're fine. And your daddy, what can I do for him? I did everything I knew to do years ago, I swear I did. And it didn't make any difference."

"It's all right, Mother," Wren said toward the window. She said it because she wanted her mother to be quiet. "We understand."

"You'll be a junior next year, Kevin," she said. "Everything happens so fast, and then we look back and wonder how the years slip away like they do. Why, I'm almost forty years old. This is a big opportunity for me. You can't know what it means."

"It means we're happy for you, Mother," Kevin said, releasing his fingers.

Chapter Three

It was over for him. Tomorrow he would hug her good-bye and she would be gone for months, maybe a year this time. Her voice would come to him over the telephone wire, and he would answer her queries about how he was and how school was going and if he needed anything. His voice was a recording, but then so was hers. They comforted each other with the familiarity, the sameness of their messages. There was never any hurt in them, no desperate whispering, no resistance.

Wren turned to them, saw the room in angles, sharp corners for puncture wounds, rectangles of slippery rugs, triangles of sharp lamplight to splinter. In a few months, her father would probably be home. He would sit molded to his familiar chair with a book on his knees, noticing the pictures from time to time when bright colors momentarily caught his eye. Or else he would stare at the television set Bliss left turned on to bring life to the room.

Wren would come to him in the late afternoon, afternoons just like this one, and find him there, not waiting for her exactly but nevertheless turning slightly toward her sound with a feebly drawn smile that told her he was glad she had come. They would sit together, not talking very much, she on the floor at his knees, while the laugh track on "The Andy Griffith Show" blared out at them sporadically and with unnatural enthusiasm for such gentle jokes.

They had nothing to say to each other, for Wren had long ago discovered that he didn't really hear her account of the day even when she embellished it, contriving stories she thought would draw his attention and make him laugh. He never laughed, and so the canned television track laughed for them; they sat together in their own quiet, separate but not, she thought, altogether alone.

It would be that way again. She knew the constancy of that life, and so she would let her mother go this time. She wouldn't cry or lie in bed tonight thinking up ploys to make Karen either stay or take them with her. There was no keeping her, any more than there was any reaching her father. There was only Kevin and her grandparents. There was music, the hours of practice that cleared her mind of everything but the distinct pattern of notes on the staff and the meter of a prescribed signature. She would make that be enough.

Chapter 4

Instead of going home after school, Wren walked in the direction of downtown. She knew the house would be empty. Karen had left that morning, dropping her off at school on her way with a feathery kiss as though it were a daily ritual between them. She had said good-bye as if she would be there waiting when the final bell clanged in the afternoon and the doors flew open against the thrust of kids rushing into the air as if one more moment inside would have suffocated them.

Once Wren would have expected to see her mother waiting there. She would have spent the whole day bound to a desk, subject after subject passing before her while her imagination took her beyond her books to Karen marketing, Karen puttering in the yard, Karen baking. But her vision was never true. Reality put Bliss in the kitchen and Karen in Atlanta in an apartment that seemed to Wren an impossibly alien place. It was where her mother slept but not where she lived. No one could actually live with those glaring white walls, chrome and glass tables and lamps, uncomfortable chairs upholstered in bold patterns against which a person's only defense was to sit on them, hiding them from view.

Today she didn't expect the Peugeot against the curb. Kevin was right. She should never even think that. Still, she couldn't go home yet; she held back for a few more hours facing her mother's absence, the unruffled quiet of the empty room where a faint scent of perfume would be lingering like an unspoken farewell written in the closed air.

She went toward the drugstore where her grandfather would be behind the raised counter, his prescription medications in giant bottles behind him. She knew he would be in his white jacket, gold-rimmed glasses pressing the bridge of his nose as he measured out tablets against a knife on his pill counter and clicked off labels on his old portable typewriter. His life was as regular as nine to five, as changeless as the lunch he ate every day sitting at the end of luncheon counter as if he were the patriarch of an endless flow of diners. He knew them all, and from noon through the afternoon there were always people browsing in the aisles waiting for their prescriptions or else sitting at the counter on coffee break from the neighboring shops. It was a friendly place, bustling and cheerful. Her grandfather was cheerful, too, always pausing to explain the details of the medication, inquiring about his customers' health, recommending patent brands, shampoos, dental floss.

The store was like home to him and the customers his friends; he never thought about retiring, although he and Bliss hadn't had a real vacation in years. They never even talked about it anymore. Unspoken between them was their responsibility to their grandchildren. And to Tom. Although Bill intended to see Kevin and Wren through college, he didn't know what the future held for his son who had not made a regular living in eight years now and didn't seem likely to ever completely support himself again.

Besides, giving up the store would mean having time to think about Tom, to dwell on all the varieties of failure he and Bliss had to live with. Working protected him from that, at least during the day; helped him concentrate on staying optimistic. It focused him on the future.

He saw Wren coming in, shrugging off her backpack as she pushed through the glass door. She'd be behind the counter in a minute, back in the medicine aisles wanting to bring him bottles, reading the alphabetized labels. She didn't work in the store yet, not like Kevin did, but she knew more about medicine than her brother, could put her hand on tetracycline as fast as her grandfather could, could pronounce the generic names and scan the reference books.

"Anything happening?" she asked him, dropping the backpack under the counter near his feet.

"These waiting," he said, pointing to a couple of loose slips on the counter. "And these to be filed." There were twenty or so prescription slips on the spindle.

"I'll file," she said.

"Get yourself a soda first. Rest a little," Bill said, looking at her over his glasses as he typed off a label. She looked tired to him. The strain of yesterday showed around her eyes.

"I don't need to rest." Wren laughed. "Don't worry about me."

"Well, get a soda then. And bring me one."

Wren went down the aisle to the lunch counter where Ginny was alternating cups under the cola fountain to keep the foam down. "Somebody was in here looking for you," Ginny said, sloshing the foam over the edge of the cup into the slotted tray beneath. "I think this stupid thing is on the blink again. Either that or it's running out already. Sometimes I think little people sneak in here at night and go on a soda binge."

"Who?" Wren asked.

"Who what?" Ginny slid the cups across the counter and smiled at the waiting customers. "Anything else for you folks?"

"Who, Ginny? Who was looking for me?"

"A young man," Ginny said, leaning back against the sandwich counter where slots held aluminum containers of salads, lettuce, pickles, sliced tomatoes. "He was tall, pretty near six feet tall, and he was wearing a navy blue jacket like the high school kids wear, and he had brown hair, a little wavy, real nice hair, and blue eyes, I think. Either blue or gray, a soft color. In fact, I thought he was real good-looking until he opened his mouth."

"What do you mean, until he opened his mouth?" Wren's fingers shook around the paper cup she held under the cola spout.

"And I saw he didn't have front teeth. Just this gaping hole."

"You're teasing me! I know you are! Now who was it?"

People along the counter were beginning to notice them, glancing furtively as they nibbled malted crackers and sucked on their straws.

"A black coffee to go, Ginny!" a man called from the cash register.

"Yessiree," Ginny said, answering both of them at the

34

same time. "He was handsome all right. Looked a lot like one of those Hollands, if you want my opinion." She took the Styrofoam cup down to the cash register, pushing the plastic lid on it as she went.

"Where'd he go, Ginny? What did you say to him?" Wren knew she was practically shouting down the counter at the woman who grinned back at her, enjoying herself.

"I told him I didn't know any Wrens." The cash register slammed shut. "And then I told him that some days, but not every day, mind you, a real cute girl comes in here and makes a nuisance of herself."

"You didn't say that!"

"Yes she did."

Wren knew without looking that it was Sam Holland who swung onto the stool in front of her. He put his elbows on the counter and rested his chin on his hands like a girl leans over an ice cream soda in magazine advertisements. He didn't look quite real sitting there looking at her, a smile beginning casually, as if they were old friends.

She watched the smile coming as if it were an event she'd been waiting for. He's smiling at me, she heard herself thinking and was suddenly afraid she'd thought it out loud. But she obviously hadn't because he wasn't looking at her now, but past her into the mirror behind the counter. For a second, his eyes acknowledged themselves, as though he had suddenly come across his own photograph in an unusual place. Then he grinned at her.

"I'm Sam Holland," he said.

"I know." Wren felt a blush rising to her cheeks. She wished her voice didn't sound so nervous and whispery. "You're a year ahead of me in school," she added to explain their connection to each other. It seemed like such a slight connection now, although she had seen him daily for all those years. He had existed for her almost as long as she could remember.

"Oh yeah. At Larkwood." He seemed embarrassed, too, as though he didn't want to remember he'd been in grade school just last year. "Good old Larkwood." He pressed the straw dispenser and three plastic straws tumbled out. He fingered one of them. "I guess I'll have a Sprite," he said.

Wren scooped crushed ice into a cup and pressed it against the lever of the machine. She could smell the syrup, a cool sweet scent, then the seltzer, but there was something else in the air, too. A kind of heat, as if her skin were growing feverish, her lingering blush turning scarlet. "Anything else?" she asked, putting the cup in front of him.

"Can you sit down?" he wanted to know. The tone in his voice was smooth again. This was his territory. It was easy for him to ask.

"I have to help my grandfather," Wren said, startled by the quickness of her excuse. Of course she wanted to join him. But something had stopped her, made her also want to turn back to the shelter of her grandfather's high counter, the familiar scent of fruity cough syrup, the bitter smell of remedies. She wanted to be eleven again so she could fantasize this moment instead of having it actually happen. She wasn't exactly sure what was happening. Something very simple for Sam Holland. She knew that much. Something he had done before because she knew these were words he was comfortable with—*come, let's, do, be*—all words of invitation.

But she hadn't learned the responses yet. *Okay* seemed like a foreign word, impossible to master on such short notice.

"Five minutes," Sam said. He put his hand out on the counter as if he intended to take hers. Even his hands knew a language she had not yet learned.

"I really can't," Wren said. She felt so stupid.

Sam's other hand dug into his pocket, and he dropped thirty-six cents on the counter. "I'll see you around then," he said. "I've got baseball practice anyway."

The coins were warm in her hand, and she clutched them like a gift she would treasure. "You were good at church," she said softly, seeing that he was disappearing. His reflection in the mirror behind her blurred as he rose.

"So were you." He sipped the Sprite once more and put it back on the counter. He buried his hands in his pockets and hunched forward a little as if he suddenly felt too tall and noticeable. "Maybe I'll see you again sometime," he said, looking slightly above her head where he could see himself playing the fool. All his confidence, the ease he'd practiced, had dissipated into this unbelievable moment of defeat.

"Sometimes I come here after school," Wren said, "but usually I go straight home. I didn't want to go home today because this morning my mother went back to Atlanta where she lives and I just couldn't stand to be there without her." She didn't understand why she was telling him all this, but she knew that it was somehow related to the sound of his voice on Sunday, the uncertainty she had heard beneath the bravado of his practiced words. "I live with my grandparents," she said.

"I know." Sam ducked his head and picked up his cup again. "Well, 'bye."

" 'Bye," Wren said, hearing regret in her voice. Perhaps he heard it, too, but if he did, he didn't let her know.

She watched him disappearing out the glass door. He stopped for a moment on the sidewalk, deciding which way to go.

Come back, she said silently, as if she expected him to somehow hear. But he was already gone.

Bliss was on her knees in the garden. She bent over, spade working the dirt as she pulled out the early shoots of weeds that would sprout up again through the mulch during the summer. It was a hopeless battle against plantain and clover, but she enjoyed being outside. This was her favorite time of day, late afternoon with the sun-warmed spring air cooling around her and the ground chilling under her knees.

She had large wet brown spots of soil on her knees and heavy damp clots of dirt clung between the fingers of her gloves. Tomorrow both pants and gloves would be dry and stiff, but she would be agile still, gratefully unhampered by the arthritic aches and lower back pain that seemed to afflict so much of her generation. She leaned back on her heels, surveying the tidy patch of tulips and jonquils she had weeded. The flowers leaned toward her, their heads dipped as if in homage to her care, although she knew their reach was toward the fading light.

She collected the pile of brush, dangling roots and ruffled edges, between her gloved hands, and rose, leaving the spade stuck in the dirt for tomorrow. She intended to work in the garden every day this spring, knowing how the steady accomplishments of her tidiness soothed her. It was work that needed doing again and again, but at least it showed more gloriously than housework.

She disliked housework, the mechanics of vacuum cleaners and electric floor scrubbers, the chemical magic of toilet cleansers and furniture polish. She had cleaned a house weekly, although frequently with hired help at her side, for forty years, and what did she have to show for it? No wax built up perhaps, but no roses either, no camellias or narcissus standing proud within her walls. The earth, not the house, was worth toiling in, worth expecting something from.

Now the house was empty. Kevin at tennis practice. Wren at the store with Bill. Karen gone without a trace, except for two children left behind. Bliss' children now. Hers and Bill's. They didn't seem to belong to Karen anymore and certainly not to Tom. They were her children, and yet they were also her connection to her son.

We should have had more children ourselves, she thought, dropping the weeds in a basket near the kitchen door. But she knew that wouldn't have made losing Tom any easier. Nothing could have lessened the guilt she'd felt all these years, the agonizing hours of soul-searching she'd spent silently replaying scene after scene between herself and her son. Where had she gone wrong?

There was no answer, only regret and a slowly born realization that the reasons didn't really matter. Her son was sick. He faced the wall of his hospital room, lost even to himself. How can I help him? she asked over and over. What can I do?

The answers seemed so simpleminded. Tell him the truth

about everything. Treat him courteously no matter how unresponsive he seems. Don't get angry or resentful. Remember that his silence is a constant cry, a terrible longing to escape the grief he feels.

But what about her grief? What about a mother's pain? Hadn't she always done all those things? Hadn't she always loved him, nurtured him, been honest with him?

In the mudroom off the kitchen, Bliss dropped her gloves on a newspaper, stepped out of her garden shoes, and slipped off her pants. Faint light studded her bare legs through the open shutters. She had good legs for a sixty-two-year-old woman. The ten pounds she'd gained over the past forty years were solid, reflecting years of tennis, hours spent walking and working in the yard. Still, she thought, tying the wraparound skirt she'd left there earlier, I've lived at least three-fourths of my life, I've taught at least ten thousand hours of piano lessons, cooked and cleaned, spent considerable time in church, on the tennis court, and at club meetings, none of which matter very much. What mattered was Tom, her failure. Her silent, spiritually paralyzed child who had found some sinister, odious kind of deliverance in his private madness.

He was not the only Jackson to lose himself. There had been Carolina, of course, who was more peculiar than sick. And Austin Jackson, Bill's uncle, who had acquired a Ph.D in English literature that he brought home to his mama's front porch where he sat every summer—he moved his chair inside in winter—and never worked a lick in his life. He claimed to be thinking, getting ready to write something down that would shake the town, then New York City, and then the world.

Chapter Four

When Austin was in his fifties he acknowledged that having an advanced degree in literature had convinced him that everything worth writing had already been committed to the printed page, and so he began considering other writers' work his own. He had autographed the public library's complete collection of Charles Dickens and was moving on to Thomas Hardy when he was caught and admonished by the librarian, who ever after frisked him for pens and pencils before letting him loose in the stacks.

The worst, of course, was young Derek Jackson, who, gone loony in the heat of the dog days, machine-gunned the street from the window of his father's third-floor office, hitting cars and parking meters while people crouched behind wheels and along curbs until Derek's father, the only general practitioner within fifty miles, shot a hypodermic needle of succinylcholine into his child's behind, right through the pants of a hundred-dollar suit, and paralyzed him.

Tom had heard those stories. Why, he'd even known Derek, Bill's older brother. Bliss had believed his knowing would protect him. She had told her grandchildren, too, recounting the stories conscientiously, as if the telling, their familiarity, would make them immune. There would be no skeletons to rattle in their closet, no unanswered questions to haunt them.

"They were eccentric," Bliss would say, "at a time when eccentricity was valued as entertainment. If your great-great-Uncle Austin hadn't commanded half the town for an audience every afternoon, he'd have gone in the house and behaved himself."

She could never let herself believe they were truly crazy.

How could she let herself think she had unwittingly married madness, not when Bill Jackson was as steady as a rock, as kind and loving as he was responsible?

Bliss turned on the faucet in the kitchen and held her hands under the warm flow. The water fell between her fingers, washing away bits of dry residue left from the inside of her gloves. She watched her hands, the water and light catching the sparkle of her rings, bubbles from the spray making tiny prisms on her wrists. The water reminded her unexpectedly of baptism.

Standing there at the sink, she saw her own immersion, the calm lake muddy around her bare feet as if disturbing it with their ceremony had literally troubled the waters. Her dress had been pale blue, the color of water. Everything had seemed blue that day—the expanse of solid, cloudless sky, the flapping hymnals the congregation held on the bank, the rinse on her mother's hair.

She had let herself be swallowed up by blueness as she opened her eyes under water and saw the light filtering through it as it swirled across her face, weighting her streaming hair and flimsy summer dress. The lake had washed away her sins, sunk every spiteful moment, every childish lie and deceit to the miry bottom like a bag of rocks. She hadn't had any big sins to wash away, at least not then. Those had come later, one tiny failing compressing itself on another until they were a hard sphere of misdeeds, like the tightly wound core of a ball, full of filthy useless dregs of fiber. Of course, the core wasn't a ball at all, but Tom who existed outside of her, unprotected and susceptible to the crush of life. She hadn't been able to save him. That was her true failing.

She turned off the water and rested her arms on the sink ledge, hands dangling wetly above the green enamel basin. She must cook dinner. Bill would be home soon, Wren in tow. Kevin would arrive exhilarated, she hoped, by two hours of successful tennis practice. They would sit together at the table in front of the dark window, the glowing light above their heads like a beacon to remind them that this was where they each belonged. Here, together, but with a generation missing. There would be no extra places, though. No obvious reminders that once there had been six places for Sunday dinner. And yet, they would all remember because there was no washing away memory. Karen would be there. And Tom. And the inherent sadness of empty places.

Chapter 5

Kevin was smoking in the bathroom. He sat on the edge of the tub, a magazine on his knees and a cigarette stuck between his lips. The smoke wafted into his face and eyes, and so he withdrew the cigarette lazily, flipped the ash into the toilet, then took a long, deliberate drag before flipping the butt in, too.

The magazine was one of Wren's. Girls photographed at peculiar angles wearing strange outfits. Baggy or pegged pants, red and yellow high heels, silky shirts, belts that circled their waists more than once and hung on their narrow hips. They were so bright with their hair held in shiny clasps, their lips as glossy as liquid on the page, teeth perfectly spaced and polished.

Wren didn't look like that. Neither did Melanie. Nobody he knew looked like those girls, although some tried. He had seen them wobbling on high heels down the halls at school with shoulder bags and swinging hair, breasts pushed up and out, hips compressed to a boy's shape. They were the same girls he sometimes saw in the gym as he passed. It surprised him that they all looked alike in their shorts and loose T-shirts, athletic socks, and knee pads, sweating as they lunged upward toward the volleyball or a rebound. It was as if they were chameleons, switching identities with their clothes. The locker room was as heavy with girls' magic as this bathroom was.

Wren had been in the shower before him. The tile of the tub enclosure was still damp and the curtain beaded with warm water. He had come into her fog as if it were a place of solace where the smells of soap and powder lay in the warm thick air waiting to envelope him and calm his ragged nerves.

He had brought the cigarette in his pocket, too, just in case the balance of warmth and scent wasn't enough. But he'd lit the cigarette right away, blowing smoke into the steamy air and following its trail toward the fogged mirror.

If he looked in the mirror, he wouldn't see himself any more than he could find Wren in the bathroom steam or Melanie in the magazine or his mother in any singular thought that made her whole to him, a complete person willing to show him how to fill in the spaces in himself and become visible in the glass.

Sometimes he wished Wren were older than he. They could change places, she be sixteen with confusion spinning in her brain while he was thirteen again, content at Larkwood School and unhampered by the embarrassments and apprehensions that threatened him.

He could possibly lose the tennis match on Friday. He had drawn Westhaven's powerhouse, a junior with long legs and arms and a bold net attack. He had seen the guy play, looked him straight in the face after a winning match and seen there, even in victory, a hungry look, aggressive and tireless. If Kevin didn't feel right, if he had to struggle too much or was slow finding his stride, this guy would cream him.

He wished he hadn't smoked the cigarette. Guilt crept over him, as it always did when he broke training. He could remember his grandmother saying to a neighbor once, "Kevin doesn't have to be reprimanded. He punishes himself."

She was right. Once he drank three beers in a row and threw up. When he was seven he climbed the forbidden elm tree in Mrs. Baker's sideyard and tore his best pants. He always trapped himself like that. His failings were thorns pricking inside his head.

At least he wasn't smoking pot. He had never even tried it, weighing, as he always did, temptation against the doom of discovery. So much was expected of him, more than he could muster even with his mind clear. Of course, not having any friends who smoked helped. The truth was he didn't have friends anymore, except for Melanie and the guys on the tennis team. Lately he hadn't cared about being with people, but it wasn't because he felt better than anyone else. Just different, more wary of the future and more alert to its pitfalls.

He had only to read the paper or listen to the news to know that the world was no longer the rich place his dad had grown up in, full of electrical gadgetry, 350-horsepower engines, elegant trains, a lit-up White House. No, the coming world would be dark, full of shadowy crowds, hungry, glazed-eyed people. How could he survive in such a place when his dad couldn't resist those little bits of darkness that crouched in the corners of a brightly lit electronic age?

Kevin dropped the magazine on the floor and got up. The condensation on the mirror was dripping now, running glossy streaks on the glass. He picked up the towel Wren had left on the rack and brought it to his face. It was cool and heavy with clean-smelling damp. He lifted his face from it and brought the towel to the mirror. In two quick wipes he could see himself, the blurred features of a solemn, dark, lean face. People thought he was handsome—his grandmother, Melanie, a slew of ninth-grade girls. But he saw a gaunt face, hollow, meatless, void of the laughter he longed to hear: the silvery chuckle of his mother, the hearty bellow of his father. All he heard was the relentless pounding of his heart, a ragged sound as inhuman as a machine. He longed for a noise, any sound that would overpower the sharp, labored cadence in his chest.

"Kevin." The voice was far away. There was so much darkness between himself and the sound. "Kevin?" But it moved closer, undeterred, resisting the dark. "Kevin!"

Softer now but closer, pressed against the door. Whispered, the syllables sung like notes. "Kevin."

It was Wren.

In her bedroom they sat together on the bed, the floor strewn with clothes she had stepped out of during the past three days, corners cluttered with stuffed animals dumped on their furry heads, unjacketed records, shoes, and books.

"Why don't you clean up this mess?" Kevin asked.

His own room was neat except for the bed he never bothered to make. His dirty clothes were balled up in the hamper, tossed in from across the room, his books unopened on his desk through the afternoon and evening. The next morning he picked them up again and toted them back to school. They were a badge he wore to identify himself—student, the nation's greatest natural resource, the hope of a difficult, uncertain future. The books provided him entry into the sprawling high school building, just as colored tags permitted workers into nuclear plants. Entering seemed about as risky, too. The classroom was a vulnerable place, not so much because he frequently arrived unprepared but because he wanted to protect the harrowing, secret belief he had acquired but that his classmates and teachers showed no sign of having gleaned. Nothing in the books mattered.

Words piled on words. Algebra problems slid down the page. Anthologies sporadically showed him the inner workings of brilliant minds, just enough insight to provide him with unanswered questions. The human body was exposed in a series of transparencies in his biology book. Maybe that mattered. Maybe his body counted for something, but not his mind, except in a computer that tallied his SAT scores, telling him where he was fit to go as if he didn't know his possibilities already.

"Kevin, you're so quiet," Wren was saying. She cradled an old, sparsely furred rabbit in her arms. "Of course there's nothing wrong with being quiet, but sometimes I feel like you're not with me anymore. Do you know what I mean?"

"Nope." He wanted to smile at her. She deserved something, an award for her perseverance through their mother's visit.

She had been so careful to be pleasant, so eager to please. She'd played the piano for Karen, that Scarlatti thing she'd been practicing for months, a difficult piece that Karen probably didn't know was so taxing.

Chapter Five

Karen had listened, sitting absolutely still on the sofa beside him, but he knew she hadn't really heard. She hadn't felt a tugging pride that this was her child who performed so difficult a feat with such grace, her narrow shoulders bent to the task, fingers perfectly curved, attention so grave and professional. Karen hadn't released that trembling sigh you would expect, that proud exultation of a parent, but had simply said, "How lovely," as if a perfect stranger had performed for her.

Only he and Bliss knew the hours Wren had spent perfecting those notes. He could hear the melody in his head, as familiar as a popular tune. Wren had given him that, he who had no talent in music, whose voice sounded straggly and alone even in a group, whose anxious childish fingers had struggled futilely to find the right piano keys until his grandmother finally gave up on him, probably as frustrated by his lack of ability as he was.

But Wren had given him music. Because of her, it meant more to him than records and tapes alone could ever make him feel. The sound of the piano live in the house sometimes exhilarated him; at other times it comforted him, reminding him of the Nietzsche quote Bliss had taped inside the door of the music cabinet: *Without music, life would be a mistake.* He didn't know who Nietzsche was, but he liked the words. The possibility of mistakes seemed so acute to him.

"I know Mother hurt you," Wren was saying. She leaned back against the headboard, her legs stretched out toward him. Her bare foot pressed against his knee, toes digging slightly.

I will make you see me, she was thinking, because Kevin

49

had not heard her yet. She knew he was listening to himself instead, hearing ominous sounds she knew nothing about. The withdrawn look on his face frightened her, and so she nudged him again with her foot.

"I know there's something between you and Mother, just like there's always been a feeling between Daddy and me. Even with him sick, I still feel close to him. I mean, I always know he's my father and I'm not ashamed of him or anything. Sometimes I get angry with him, though. I could never really get angry with Mother, I don't think. Do you know what I mean?"

She obligated him to answer her. He could remember hating her, days when the nuisance she made of herself irritated him to the point of wanting to hit her. Sometimes he had. A passing slap on the arm, nothing he could be blamed for, nothing she would complain about. But he had felt a connection to her at those moments of frustration, just as strong as now. He had always known they had to stay together, two fragments of a passion that neither of them could remember or understand. A lost love.

"I would have gone with her if she'd wanted me," Kevin said.

"You wouldn't have," Wren said. "I know you wanted her to ask, but you wouldn't have gone when the time came. Leave Melanie and school? Leave Grandmother and Granddaddy? Me? I don't believe you."

"I would have, I swear it." Kevin grabbed her foot and squeezed it hard, expecting her to squeal or struggle away.

She didn't.

He pressed his fingers into the tender arch of her foot. He could feel the tendons, the knobs of bone beneath his thumb. "I would have, Wren. You better believe it."

He let go her foot, and she drew it up under her, protecting herself from him.

"I hurt you, didn't I?" he asked, his voice softening as he nodded toward the foot she'd covered with her knee. "I'm sorry."

"Just forget about it, Kevin." Wren's eyes looked glassy, and she dropped the rabbit on the bed between them as if she felt compelled to abandon comfort in an overt show of strength.

He picked up the rabbit. It was from another life, an Easter so long ago that he couldn't even remember it. A time when they must have lived together in the house on Statler Street. There would have been eggs to find in the pale spring grass and new shoes. Wren had probably worn a white bonnet sprinkled with tiny flowers and a shiny ribbon knotted at the ends and tied beneath her chin. They must have made such a pretty picture.

"If I went, you would go with me," he said, looking down at the frayed rabbit. "I guess we're in this together."

"She'll never ask us now, Kevin. You know that. You've always told me that." Wren put out her hand as if to touch the rabbit, but her fingers found his and she pressed them.

"I know," he said, attempting to smile at her. His face looked crooked. "I guess I just needed to choose for myself. You know, take a position on my own, for myself."

"But this isn't like a battle. There aren't any sides, Kevin. We don't have enemies."

"I think," Kevin said, releasing her hand so that they seemed to drift quickly away from each other, "it would be better if we did."

Chapter 6

Sometimes the phone rings differently. How else did Wren know to spring ahead of Kevin in the upstairs hall and then pause a moment to collect herself, the silent receiver against her breathless chest? Why else would she shut her eyes tight, blocking out Kevin's impatient frown to see in the blue glare of her squint, a picture of Sam Holland?

"Hello," she said and waited to hear him answer.

"Wren?"

"Yes, this is she." Still Kevin frowned at her but he was beginning to turn away, smacking the railing with his jacket as he left for his tennis match.

"It's Sam," the voice said, but it wasn't his voice.

It wasn't either of his voices, not the one that had touched her two Sundays ago, reaching out to pull her along; not the casual, confident one that had stunned her in the drugstore. This was another voice, so close she could feel it. She could see his face, too, as she would if she were a prisoner and they faced each other from either side of a thick forbidding partition of glass. She put both hands on the receiver to keep from reaching out to touch him.

"I'm glad I found you." He paused, startled by the

double meaning he'd not expected to hear. "I called down at the drugstore. They told me you'd gone to Jolene's so I called there. . . ." There was silence.

"I'm glad you found me, too," Wren said, not wanting to let that thought get away.

"Right," Sam said. "Listen, I'm calling about tomorrow. My dad is going over to the Reed Farm to do some work, and I thought you might want to come along. I know it sounds strange, but the Reed Farm is a nice place and. . . . Do you think you can? We could pick you up about nine, and Mom said she'd pack us some sandwiches. What do you think?"

What did she think? In a moment that stretched across her whole life, she saw Saturday mornings: the quiet, dreadful breakfasts, the careful armoring as she and her grandmother dressed, the familiar road and billboards along the way, the songs they sang to lock out the fear. She saw her father's chalky cheeks, his drawn mouth, his useless hands. Could this Saturday be different? Could she make it different? Should she?

And then, how could she not? It would be like refusing spring. But wouldn't that be selfish? Wouldn't the spring in her bloom year after year? And yet, how could she wait another season, give up this voice so close to her ear?

"I'll come," she said.

"We'll be there at nine," Sam answered. "Wear Levi's and old shoes." He paused as if waiting for her to answer him again. "Wren?"

"I'm here," she said.

"I'll see you tomorrow."

"Tomorrow, at nine."

"In Levi's and old shoes."

"Yes."

"Well, good-bye."

"Good-bye."

But she held on to the phone to hear the connection break. The wire hummed, but she heard his voice on it. *I found you,* he had said. *Come.*

All week she had been expecting just those words. She had been preparing herself for them, sensing their imminence. She had practiced her yes as if it were a new language, because it was. Her life had been spent saying no. No, I don't need you. No, I can manage myself. No, don't come with me. They were the answers her parents required.

Still she held the phone, connected to the sound of Sam Holland's voice. "Yes," she said to the hum. "Yes, I'll come. Yes."

Melanie Washburn was waiting outside the locker room. She leaned against the cool wall, shoulders back like a statue, immobile except for the occasional itchy twitching of her nose. She had hay fever. Every spring her eyes watered, her nostrils and the roof of her mouth reddened and itched, her sinuses alternately flowed and stopped up. April was agony with pollen powdering the air and damp soil breeding mold. This afternoon the basement hallway seemed especially dank after the hot sun outside, and Melanie shivered as she rubbed her hands on her arms.

"Oh, hurry up," she said between her teeth while a sneeze made its itchy way through her nasal passages.

"I'm ready," Kevin said, coming down the hall toward her. There was a bounce in his step and he was swinging his tennis bag so it swished against his leg with his stride. "I'm starving!"

"To the victor go the spoils," Melanie said. She took the jacket he handed her and wrapped it around her shoulders.

"Hamburgers! Three hamburgers all the way, large fries, a vanilla shake!" Kevin shouted as if he expected sustenance to appear out of thin air at his command. He stopped and pulled Melanie close to him. "And then we'll go some-where."

"More spoils, huh?" Melanie laughed and then sneezed three times. "I can't stand it!" she moaned, searching for a tissue in her pocket. She blew her nose into it.

"Take a pill," Kevin said, pulling her along. "Take two." He hugged her hard. "I beat him, Melanie! At first I thought he had me—that net attack and his forcing me into that running backhand, but then something told me he was worried, something in his stance and the way he worked his shoulders. He wanted to win too much. It was a mental thing."

They got in the car. "We could go to the movies," Melanie suggested.

"That's where everybody's going." Kevin drove toward the nearest burger joint.

"It's air-conditioned. Two hours in air conditioning might mean I'll live," Melanie said.

"We could watch TV at my house," Kevin said. "My grandparents are going out to dinner, and Wren's probably gone somewhere, too. She got a call just before I left."

"You don't have any money," Melanie said.

"Enough for supper. Not enough for a night on the town." He swung into the parking lot and rolled down the window. "Let's eat in the car. Who needs all those people?" They could see the heads of friends who sat in the booths along the wall.

After the carhop had taken their order, Kevin closed the window again. They sat in insular silence, although the blare from the jukebox amplifier sometimes banged against their windows and friends waved at them on their way in and out. Inside the car they were quiet, recovering from victory, the heady, exhaustive joy that Kevin felt as keenly as his hunger. But they were also preparing for the night, their moments alone, a time when they would touch and say words that in this early evening light seemed impossibly intimate.

Melanie stuffed her hamburger wrapper into the paper bag and folded it closed. "Well," she said, sniffing the drying mucus in her head.

"I feel so tired now," Kevin said, "like I don't want to move for a month."

"I've heard of someone doing that—a man who lived in his car parked in a parking lot until the police finally towed him away. Everything he owned was in that car."

"He was crazy," Kevin laughed and then stopped and stared at himself in the rear-view mirror. "But then, so are we."

"You are not!" Melanie reached over to hug him. She wished he wouldn't say things like that. Sometimes his joking sounded so serious, as if his mind created a cruel image of himself that she must protect him from. She put her face against his, feeling the cool fresh skin after his shower. His cheekbone was hard against her cheek, but his ear was soft and touchable. "I love you," she whispered into that ear.

"That's nice to know," Kevin said and kissed her cheek before leaning back, away from her.

She felt him pulling away, and so she faced the window again to watch people coming out of the restaurant. She took a final crunch of ice from her cup and put it in the bag, too. "I'm ready," she said.

"We'll go home then, and see what's happening."

The lights were on, but Bliss and Bill were at the door on their way out.

"How'd it go?" Bill asked.

"He won," Melanie said.

"Yeah, well, that guy's not as good as he looks," Kevin said.

"He's the best Westhaven has and you know it. Congratulations," Bliss said, hugging him. "Wren's in her room listening to records. Just let her know you're here. We won't be late."

They went into the family room. On the paneled wall above the television were plaques and awards commemorating moments of glory in their past—Bill's military service medals, his local Man of the Year award, certificates of appreciation for civic work, gifts from Bliss' piano students, a shelf of her tennis trophies. His parents' wedding picture, a casual photo, windblown and laughing, unlike the solemn formal portrait of Karen in the living room. A studio portrait of Bliss and Bill with their grandchildren. Here we are. This is all of us, their smiles said.

His father's medals were there, too. Shining medallions awarded him at forensic competitions when he was in high school and college. Tom Jackson had been quick of tongue, glib. But he'd learned to write and deliver arguments, had made his points consistently, each blow punctuated with his natural humor and style. He had charmed his audience as much as convinced them, Bliss said.

Kevin sat down and watched the lamplight glinting on the metal surfaces. Cups glittered, figures poised for action caught the light along their slender curves, plaques gleamed, glass shimmered. He had cups of his own there, small ones beside Bliss'. Junior tournaments at the country club and from the summer recreation program. Then Wren's music awards, achievement ratings in calligraphy behind glass. Year after year she was willing to put her solitary, relentless practicing to the test by traveling anxious miles to recital halls. He had been with her, and so he knew how slowly the minutes passed in soundproof practice rooms behind stages. Then there was the glare of the empty stage with its monstrous piano waiting to spit out every irregular rhythm, every hesitant flight of fingers.

They were a competitive family with a wall to prove it. Everybody did his best, and Bliss was there to see to it. Cheerfully, confidently, his grandmother guided them on, nudged them carefully toward their natural abilities. She had probably done the same with his father, and look where it had taken him.

"What is it, Kevin?" Melanie asked, and he remembered she was there. "Let's call Wren down here and play cards or something."

"I don't want to." He sounded so angry, his voice slicing

into the silence, although he hadn't intended to sound angry. He went and sat beside Melanie on the sofa. "I mean, I just want to be with you for a while." He took her hand and pressed his fingers between hers. They fitted. "I don't need anybody but you." Their faces were moving together.

"Kevin, I think I'm going to sneeze."

Noses touched.

"Well, don't," Kevin said and kissed her.

Bliss was drinking milky tea in the kitchen. She had come down the stairs quietly, holding the skirt of her bathrobe above her ankles as she came. Then down the dark hall, the carpet warm against her bare feet, and into the kitchen where she switched on the light above the stove and heated the kettle. The kettle sang softly, and she poured water out over a tea bag in her cup, dipped the bag deeply in and out, then dropped it in the sink and poured milk in the cup. She wanted sugar, too, but would forego it, although her memory of the taste of the milky hot water with sugar her mother used to drink at night was with her like a visitor.

She remembered sleepless nights long ago when she was a girl and would come down to find her mother still about, curled on the sofa with a book or in the kitchen at a table much like this one, having toast and a hot drink. They had talked then, while the house clucked and sighed around them. Her mother had given her absolute attention, her book closed on her lap, and so in the night unexpected words had passed between them, mother and child, as they spoke of minute concerns, daily worries that hampered them, the wistful dreams of girls, the unquenchable hopes of mothers.

Bliss missed her mother now at the table in her own kitchen. It would be so good to hear that voice again as it went gently but unerringly to the truth of the matter at hand. She would offer advice couched in experience but would not expect it to be heeded. But I'm almost as old as she was when she died, Bliss thought, and where is the experience I need for this?

"Bliss?" It was Bill in the hallway. He came into the light, rubbing his hands up his cheeks and over his eyes. "What time is it?"

"Three o'clock," Bliss said.

Bill sat down across from her and rested his head on one hand.

"You can't see a thing, can you?" Bliss laughed softly.

"Very little," Bill answered. "After all these years I still wake up with the idea that in a minute my eyes will clear and I'll be able to see perfectly without my glasses. Vanity, I suppose, catches unsuspecting souls."

"Or hope springs eternal." Bliss got up to make him tea.

"This is bad for us." Bill stirred sugar into his cup.

"It's mostly hot water, the kind of weak tea Mama used to drink late at night."

"What are you doing down here, anyway?"

"Thinking. Did Wren tell you she's going out to the Reed Farm with John Holland's son in the morning? I'm glad. It'll be good for her to have an outing."

"That's what's keeping you awake?"

"Of course not." Bliss got up and took a letter from the drawer of her kitchen desk. "This came this morning. I didn't tell you because we were going out to dinner and I knew there wouldn't be time to talk about it then." She held out the letter to him, but he didn't take it. "It's from Karen." Bliss put the letter in her pocket. "She's getting a divorce. I think she intended to tell us when she was here but she couldn't bring herself to say it, although I don't see why not. She already acts divorced."

"Bliss."

"I know, I know. But I have to say it, at least to you." She sat down at the table and laid her hands out flat on its surface. They were such strong hands, adept at five-finger exercises, gripping tennis rackets, planting things. Now they seemed to be trembling. "She can get a divorce in thirty days because she and Tom haven't lived together in all these years. I don't think there's anyone else. I suppose it's just unfinished business she wants finished before she goes."

"Can you blame her?" Bill asked. He was watching Bliss' hands, unable to look at her face. He knew in the blur of features across from him, he would see grief and the fuzzy outline of pain.

"Yes, Bill! Yes, I can blame her! It was in sickness and in health, wasn't it? For better or for worse?"

"But he's not the man she married, Bliss. We can't deny that."

"And he isn't the son I raised, but I love him still. I see him as helpless as an infant. I see him struggling to stand, to walk—God help us—to speak. Over and over again I see him fail, those terrible slow slides into defeat. But I still love him, Bill. You still love him. His children still love him."

"What will you tell them?" Bill asked.

"The truth, as gently as I can. But heaven only knows what they'll hear and what it will mean to them."

"Take a little time. Maybe there'll be a moment that seems just right."

"Maybe." Bliss got up and put their cups in the sink.

"Can you sleep now?" Bill put his arm around her shoulder.

"I hope so." She slipped her arm around his waist. She felt so weary, tired to the bone with the gloom of tomorrow's thankless visit weighting her, exhausted by the task at hand. She must tell the children. It was so hard.

The hall upstairs was quiet and bathed in light from the lamp they left burning. Wren's light, they once had called it, but now it was everybody's light, making visible a familiar place that in pitch black would be so foreign. "Give me something to see by," Wren had said. And so they had provided this little lamp.

Her arm around her husband, Bliss passed the light, throwing a curving shadow across the stair, and went into their room where the white comforter on their bed shone dimly and the tulips from her garden dipped golden in their slender vase. She had come to this room so many years ago, a time almost as distant as when she'd sat with her mother in another house and closed up the space between them with women's talk. And now here was Bill, as dependable as the solid walls he'd built for her, as warm as the bed they crawled into, as dear as any memory.

"I love you, Bliss," a voice said in the dark.

Then a cool foot rested against hers, and there was no accounting for the joy of it.

Chapter 7

John Holland's truck turned off the highway onto a wide, smooth gravel road and went through a bar gate left open for them. Wren and Sam stood on the bed of the truck and leaned backward against the cab, gripping the wooden rails for balance.

Wren was glad they were riding in the open instead of in the cab with Mr. Holland. She wouldn't have known what to say to him, although he'd given her a friendly wave when she came down the walk with Sam and had smiled at her through the rear window before starting the truck. He didn't seem to mind her coming along.

Still she wouldn't know what to say to him, any more than she knew what to say to his son now that he was next to her. Fortunately, the wind had blown their tentative attempts at conversation away, and so she only glanced at Sam occasionally, smiled when their eyes met, and then looked out again at the spring morning that appeared in splashes of light and color in the woods—dogwoods and redbuds punctuating the new yellow-green of the poplars among the heavy shades of the evergreens.

She had seldom been on this road and was surprised that

the terrain just twenty miles from town could have rises in it, little hills rolling forward and inclines at the crest of which the morning seemed to spread out, completely visible. She wanted to swing her arms out and take it in, wrap the day in her expectations to make it truly perfect, but she held on. The truck jostled on the gravel, and she watched the trail of dust like a murky wake rising behind them.

"Look!" Sam said into her ear, and she turned first to him and then to the sight toward which he pointed.

The Reed Farm sparkled. Sun touched the pastures, burnished the coats of the horses, glared off the white fences and the house, a gigantic house with a porch across it and red awnings on all the windows. To the left, set back from the house, was a white stable with a training ring in front of it, and to the right, almost hidden in the woods, was a new barn, not yet stained so that the raw wood seemed golden, washed in its own special blend of sunlight.

"It's perfect," Wren said, although Sam couldn't hear her.

He could see her smile, though. It was what he'd hoped for, a smile that wasn't hesitant or embarrassed like the glances she'd been giving him, not uneasy as she'd seemed when she'd opened the front door to him and then shut it quickly behind her, as though she were closing herself back in and only a shadow of herself, an expendable layer, was coming with him. For a few minutes, he'd thought he shouldn't have invited her. It was a dumb date; at least most girls would think so. He had counted on Wren's being different.

The truck came to a halt on the road beside the house,

and John Holland blew the horn one solemn blast. They waited while the dust rose and settled around the truck. Then the back door opened, and a woman wearing a bathrobe came out.

"Hello, John," she said, shading her eyes with her hand. "Reed's up there at the new barn, him and a lot of other people. Looks like they intend to make a party out of it. Traffic's been coming by here like this is a highway. You had breakfast?"

"Sure have, but thanks anyway, Ida," John Holland said. "I'll go on up there."

"We beat Griffin High yesterday," Sam said to Wren. "Seven to three. I got a triple in the fifth."

"That's good," Wren said, although she was trying to overhear the conversation below.

"You weren't there, were you? I didn't see you," Sam said.

"I don't go to many games. I never have time." She forced a smile. "Maybe I'll go to some next year," she added.

"Don't you start without me," Mrs. Reed was saying.

"Don't start what?" Wren whispered. There was an odd note of belligerence in her voice, as if she'd become ill at ease without knowing it.

"I've just got to throw on some clothes and I'll be up there." Mrs. Reed went back into the house as the truck started up.

"Don't do what without her?" Wren asked again, hanging on to the railing as the truck turned slowly up a bumpy road toward the barn.

"You'll see," Sam said. "We've got a great team this year.

The newspaper says it's the best team we've had since we won the championship in seventy-four. A fifteen-and-four season so far."

Several trucks were parked beside the barn; men were leaning against them, talking and drinking coffee out of thermos cups. They were wearing their Saturday-in-town clothes as if this were an occasion, and obviously they knew what the occasion was. Unless Mrs. Reed came, Wren would be the only female there, and she had come without question, simply because Sam Holland asked her. How could she have done that, she wondered, deserting Bliss to a lonely drive to the hospital when she didn't even know this person, much less like him?

She jumped off the back of the truck when it stopped and followed Sam, who was carrying a six-pack of cola.

"I'm going to put these drinks in your cooler, Mr. Reed, if that's all right," he called to a burly man in a pressed Big Mac worksuit.

"Help yourself, son," Mr. Reed said as he shook hands with John Holland.

Wren watched Sam putting the cans in the cooler. She felt deserted already, abandoned to a day of misery because she had trusted the intentions of someone she hardly knew. She didn't know anything about baseball. She didn't even care about baseball. She didn't care about Sam Holland, either. Why had she come?

"Glad you could make it, John," Mr. Reed was saying. "It's turned out to be a good day. I guess you see you're going to have an audience. Mostly believers, I think. Folks from this end of the county. Thought some of them might be calling on you themselves."

"Wren, bring that sack, will you? It's in the cab," Sam called to her.

Wren brought the grocery bag to him. "What are we doing here?" she asked while he looked in the sack.

"Cherry tomatoes, potato salad, cupcakes. I knew Mom wouldn't just send sandwiches." He put the sack in the cooler on top of the drinks and shut it.

"What are we doing here?" Wren asked again. She could feel tension in her shoulders.

"Don't you have a lick of patience, girl?" Sam asked, grinning at her. "I bet you read the last page of a mystery before you even start it."

Mr. Holland was walking alone out into the woods that bordered the field where the barn stood. Watching his slow, purposeful movement, Wren could see how alike he and Sam were. They were both slow, steady, confident.

"Where's he going?"

"To get his equipment," Sam said, holding back a chuckle. Any minute now Wren would know what they'd come for.

"What kind of equipment?" she asked. Maybe Sam's bringing her had been a joke. Maybe at school Monday he'd get a laugh out of how he'd brought her out to a farm. A cheap date, he'd say, if he called it a date at all. She wished she'd gone to the hospital. At least it was familiar. She knew what to expect there—no impatience, no resentment, no misunderstanding, just sedated calm. At the hospital she would be practically devoid of feeling, not like here where she felt flushed with embarrassment and apprehension.

"What kind of equipment? I want to know, Sam."

John Holland was returning, a flowering dogwood branch

in one hand and his knife in the other. He sat down on the tailgate of the truck and began stripping the branch of its foliage. The white bracts holding the tiny green buds fell around him.

The men watching fell silent around her.

"Tell me what he's doing," Wren whispered, real anger finally in her voice. It was so unfair of him not to tell her.

"He's making a divining rod," Sam said quietly. "See, it's a branch with two branches growing from it so that it forms a Y."

"But what's he going to do with it?" Wren asked.

"Do you remember the story of the Israelites in the wilderness? They rose up against Moses because of their great thirst, and so God said to Moses, 'Behold I will stand before thee there upon the rock of Horeb; and thou shalt smite the rock, and there shall come water out of it, that the people may drink.'"

"You mean he's going to find water?" Wren cried and then clasped her hand over her mouth.

"If there's any to be found," John Holland said over his shoulder to her.

"But isn't there another way?" Wren whispered to Sam. "A more scientific way?"

"Dad doesn't think so. He's been dowsing for years, ever since he was a little boy and his own daddy put the rod in his hands. He's got a pretty good record, too." Sam laughed. "I know you don't know what to think right now, but keep your mind open, will you? This is just one of those things that can happen if you believe."

How can he be so sure of everything, Wren wondered, when he's just a year older than me? Hasn't he ever felt his confidence snagged against experience like I have? You couldn't have a father in and out of mental hospitals without wondering about yourself. Wren knew how little it took to make a person collapse, confidence shredded into panic. She knew something about frailty even if Sam didn't.

The men were beginning to talk again, leaving John Holland to his preparations.

"I saw a man dowsing once," one of them said. "He was using rods—copper, I think they were—and when he came to a certain place, those rods opened so one was pointing due east and the other due west. That's where they drilled—right where he was standing—and they had themselves a well. Had ten gallons a minute, too, but it wasn't fit to drink. Iron water. Still, the man found it."

"I've got a better one," another man said, looking around to see who was listening.

Wren leaned against the truck and looked off toward the house as if she were paying attention to Mrs. Reed, who, dressed now in jeans and a bright shirt, was coming up the lane.

"There was this man divining, using a Y branch just like John's fixing there, and he found water with it. So then some other folks wanted to try it, and the dowser let 'em. I remember"—the man was beginning to laugh—"I remember the dowser says to this one fella, now don't you be walking fast, else you might get hurt. But that fella didn't pay no attention, and he took off holding that branch so it was pointed straight up in the air and he was just about running with it when *Wham!* down comes that rod and hits him right between the legs! Smack in his privates! I swear, it was the beatingest thing I ever saw! That fella was lying there on the ground, hurt bad, and the dowser, he was an old man then and long dead now, he said, 'I told you not to run, boy.' We laughed. I declare it was a sight. But I tell you one thing, everybody else that tried dowsing walked real slow."

Ida Reed had reached the barn and was standing with her husband. "I told Reed we could run a line over here from the house," she said. "But he wanted a new well. Got a new barn, got to have a new well to go with it. So I said, call up the drilling company and get them out here. But he said they'd put holes all over this field before they ever got a good one. He was already planning to call you, John."

"Well," John Holland said, "we'll see what we can do." He slid off the truck, the double-pronged branch in his hand. "What was it you had in mind, Reed?"

"Something between eight and ten gallons is enough. I don't expect you'll find a dome out here. A good running vein would do it."

"Well, let's get at it," John said and went back to the edge of the woods behind the barn, his silent audience trailing after him.

"I hope you're ready for this," Sam said to Wren. "We can stand on the truck if you want to."

"No, I want to see up close," she said, moving away from Sam to follow the men. Finding water with a stick didn't seem as impossible to her as being with Sam Holland did. She could be on her way to the hospital right now, Bliss close beside her, their voices fitting together. Instead she was here, a misfit because the connection she'd felt between herself and Sam Holland two Sundays ago had been a mistake. A mistaken identity. She had thought he'd had some experience comparable to hers, maybe not a sick father or an absent mother, but some other moment of doubt when what was expected of him was more than he could possibly do.

The sun was suddenly high and hot. Ida Reed fanned herself with a sycamore branch, and Mr. Reed sweated through the back of his Big Mac worksuit. Only John Holland seemed cool, oblivious of his surroundings except for the earth beneath him. Holding the branch by its curved ends with the first three fingers of each hand, palms up so that the straight end was in front of his face, he began walking slowly in a straight line along the edge of the clearing.

"I am looking for a vein of potable water," he said to the ground. "I am looking for a vein of potable water." Again and again he repeated the sentence, moving slowly, the branch still upright in his hands.

He reached the lower corner of the field and then turned back toward the woods, moving in closer to the barn a few feet. About halfway in toward the crowd that waited at the other end of his route, the rod began to move, twisting forward in his hands. He took another slow step and the branch pulled downward, trembling slightly against the pull of his fingers to keep it upright.

"Mark this place, Sam," he called.

Sam pushed a long nail with a strip of cloth attached to its head into the ground.

John Holland moved off the spot and put the rod back into search position. For more than two hours he walked the field, stopping where the rod directed him, repeating over and over the purpose of his search: "I am looking for a vein of potable water." The field was spotted with bits of cloth.

"Let's stop for lunch," John said finally. He seemed to be putting the men's faces back into focus as he took off his hat and rubbed his hand across his face. Then he stretched. "I never know how worn out this makes me until I stop."

After dividing the lunch with his father, Sam took Wren into the barn where they spread their meal on the new straw. The barn was cool and held the fresh scent of new sappy wood and sweet hay.

Wren sat down on the ground, her back against a stall, and bit into the sandwich Sam handed her. "I'm so hungry," she said, tucking a loose sprig of lettuce into her mouth.

"So am I. Hard work does that to me." Sam popped the cap off a can of soda and handed it to her.

"What have you done?"

"Concentrated. Nobody knows how dowsing works. We just know it does, and that it's serious. I mean, you couldn't go out there joking around and necessarily find anything. Of course, you might. But probably not. You have to have confidence in it, I guess. Of course, people have been dowsing for thousands of years. That's proof there's something to it. Dad's proof, too. He always finds water. It might not be the water you're looking for, and sometimes the depth isn't right, but he'll find it. I tell you one thing, it'll be the best hundred dollars Mr. Reed ever spent, and he'll tell you so himself."

"What will your dad do now that he's found water in so many places?"

"He'll try to find the best vein. From the look of the stobs I'd say there's a place where two veins cross. That'll be the strongest flow. Then, next week, the drilling company will come out, and we'll know for sure. It's just got to be fairly close to the surface and, of course, it's got to be good water."

"Potable."

"Exactly. You're catching on!"

"Seeing's believing," Wren said, forking potato salad out of a plastic cup.

"I'm seeing you right now, but I'm not sure I should believe it," Sam said. "I can't believe you actually came."

The tone in his voice made Wren look up to see that he'd stopped eating and was looking at her. She recognized this voice. It seemed compatible with hers, familiar, as if he'd just clicked into a different key.

"I used to see you," she said after a moment. "All through school you were always ahead of me, being absolutely perfect. Best athlete, best student, best every-thing. I guess you still are."

"It was easier in grade school," Sam said.

"But you're still so confident about everything."

"I have to work at it. Everybody does."

"I don't believe you."

"Sometimes I feel good about what I'm doing. I feel hot, you know, and I can tell while I'm shooting that the basket's good or I know the bat's going to connect. But it's not always like that."

"I don't know anything about sports," Wren said. "No, that's not exactly true. I just don't care about them, except for swimming. I like to watch tennis. I'm not very competitive, I guess, not like you are."

"I don't believe that," Sam said.

"Well, it's true. I play the piano but when I'm

practicing, I'm playing against myself. I want to improve, not beat somebody else."

"But you go to competitions," Sam argued.

"How did you know that?"

"I know a lot about you. I know your mother lives in Atlanta—you told me. I know your father is sick most of the time. You live with your grandparents. I know Kevin. I think you believe my dad can find water."

Wren wanted to answer, but she didn't want to argue with the new gentleness in his voice.

"Wait," he said and took her hand. "I know when you were singing in church, my heart was pounding."

"You were nervous."

"Not until you sang, I wasn't. I was looking at you, the side of your face just like now, but you seemed miles away. There was no reaching you." He sighed and rolled his head back against the stall. "Then I had to get up and talk—"

"It was a wonderful talk." Wren smiled, remembering. She had felt close to him toward the end. It was the same feeling she had now.

"It was dumb. I kept hearing myself say that crap and I knew how dumb it was. I was really thinking about you. Wondering what you were thinking. I wanted to impress you, I guess." Sam squeezed her fingers lightly but looked away from her. "Then I came to the drugstore and it was terrible."

"I didn't know what to say." Wren looked down at his hand over hers. "I still don't. I'm not good at this."

"But you came today. I really wanted you to." He was looking at her now. "I guess I wanted you to see my dad doing this weird thing. I thought it would help."

74

"Help what?"

"My case, I guess. I guess I thought you weren't going to go for my macho stuff."

"So this is the real Sam Holland?"

"I don't know." He released her hand and ran his fingers across her wrist. "Is this the real Wren Jackson?" He had found her pulse.

"No fair." She laughed, pulling her hand free. It was hard not to like him.

They could hear the men gathering in the field.

"I think it's time to find potable water," Wren said, going to the open gate of the barn. "Let's go watch."

"Okay," Sam said, following her. "But I think I've already found what I'm looking for."

Chapter 8

Despite Bill's comforting words, Bliss knew there would be no good time to tell Kevin and Wren that their mother had started divorce proceedings. But still she waited through the weekend and into the first week in May, days easing toward Mother's Day when her grandchildren would bring her gifts. Costume jewelry, a returnable blouse from Broadhurst's Department Store, cards decorated with cartoon figures and acknowledging their affection in silly verse.

Once their gifts had all come from the drugstore shelves —dusty bottles of cologne, a set of steak knives, a battery-operated wall clock in the shape of an apple, a wooden candlestick surrounded by a ring of artificial violets. The cards had been sentimental then, adorned with pink roses in hazy light, their accolades in florid script. The cards had embarrassed Bliss a little, had even made her teary because she knew the care with which they had been selected. She could see Wren hunched in front of the card display conscientiously reading the words, searching for the most lavish praise, the headiest arrangement of angels and flowers. At eight, Wren had meant what her card said and had even added her own carefully spaced *I love you* under the rhyme and then a row of *x*'s to mark a multitude of kisses.

Kevin's cards had been similar but less sentimental, more homey. A picture of an old-fashioned kitchen, wooden spoons in a decorated enamel pitcher, or a rosy, aproned grandmother surrounded by cherubic children. He only signed his name.

Now the cards were silly, Ziggy's dumpy shape, Snoopy's sentiments. They suited Bliss better because they seemed careless, unhampered by responsibilities. They made her laugh.

She had to remind them to select cards for Karen. She knew it was difficult to find a verse that didn't announce gratitude for care, devotion, constancy. And the gifts— what to give a mother who has everything? They sent her hanging baskets to hide the stark open space of her windowed walls. Popular novels. Monogrammed stationery. Photographs of themselves.

On the Saturday before Mother's Day, Bliss and Wren went to see Tom in the hospital. He was wearing clothes now—worn khaki slacks, a soft loose summer shirt, and his slippers, but no belt because belts were forbidden. Wren could see he was better.

"Here's my girl," he said to his roommate, who was new and who lay motionless on the bed across the room. The man looked like Tom had looked a month ago, as empty as a shell, faceless.

Tom was smiling, but his smile struggled nervously on his gaunt face. Getting better always keyed him up. It was a risky business, fraught with the possibility of a setback from some unexpected source. The color of the sky one morning could make him weary. The ceiling could crawl with forbidding shapes. His dinner could nauseate him.

"Daddy," Wren said and went to kiss him. His cheek was loose and boneless as if his skeleton had shrunk while his flesh held its own shape. She pressed her lips to the bone.

One hand went up to touch her. "Wren," he said. "Mother."

Bliss bent to his chair to kiss him, too, and then took his hand. "You're so much better," she said.

"Yes." His smile failed. "Didn't Kevin come?"

"He wanted to," Bliss said, "but Bill needed him at the store." The lie seemed so familiar. At this point in every recovery Tom noticed Kevin's absence, and always Bliss furnished the same excuse.

"So he's working." Tom nodded, remembering. "That's good."

"And you're eating," Bliss said. "I think you've gained weight this week."

"The food is bad," Tom said. "Not like your grandmother's," he said to Wren.

"Well, it's institutional food," Bliss said. "You can't expect much."

"Edible, maybe," Tom said and smiled at his little joke.

"When you come home, we'll make all your favorite things, won't we, Grandmother? Spinach lasagne, chocolate cream pie, chicken in wine sauce. Steaks on the grill." Wren could see the meals. She imagined her father at the table, his appetite suddenly ravenous, his voice booming over them. She had a memory of that sound, but she knew she had probably dreamed it and then gradually weighted the dream down, sharpened its soft corners with her imagination until it had become real.

"It may be a while yet," Tom said. His hands were curled uneasily in his lap, nails blunt and clean, fingers lax and soft.

"But you're so much better, Daddy," Wren said. "I know you are."

Bliss could see him escaping. His eyes focused above their heads on the blank wall, his hands fell slowly apart, his shoulders slipped forward.

"It takes time, Wren," she said and took her son's hands between her own, pressing them back into place. "You have lots of time, Tom."

That was how the minutes always turned against them so that time became the enemy. If only they could stop the day, hold the sun in place to fight and win this battle, then they could find comfort in the cooling evening, the shadows that curled across their faces as the car moved down the shady road away from the hospital. Toward home.

The Cadillac's clock ticked, the hands moving relentlessly through the afternoon.

"I had a letter from Karen," Bliss said, her voice in cadence with the clock's ticking as if it were a metronome. "She wanted me to tell you and Kevin something. I think she wanted to tell you herself when she came last month but it was so difficult for her to tell you about the move to Chicago. You know it was hard, don't you, Wren?"

"What is it, Grandmother?" Wren held her breath as if she were about to sink into a pool of water. Drown.

"She's getting a divorce." Bliss watched the road. "It's a formality, of course. You know yourself that she and your

79

father haven't lived together for years. In a way, they've been divorced for a long time. So it's just a formality."

"Will she still come to see us?" Wren's lungs were empty, caved inward.

"Of course she will, Wren. It has nothing to do with you and Kevin. Everything will be like always. It's just that there'll be this document, this divorce decree, so she'll be free. They'll both be free." Bliss' hand left the wheel to rest on Wren's thigh.

"Daddy won't be free," Wren said.

"If he ever wanted to get married again, he could."

"But he won't. She will, though, won't she? That's what this is all about."

"We don't know that, Wren. Karen didn't say anything about the future except that she could get a divorce in thirty days in Georgia and she was going to do it."

"Thirty days? That's all it takes?"

"When a couple hasn't lived together in years, I don't imagine it takes longer than that anywhere."

"Does Kevin know?"

"I thought I'd tell you first. I've hoped I'd find a way to tell him that wouldn't be so painful, but I don't suppose there is one."

"We'll do it together," Wren said.

The roadside sped by them. Billboards advertising cars and burgers and overnight lodgings rolled out of their view.

"Let's sing something," Wren said.

The Cadillac hummed as their two voices lifted above the cacophonous anguish they felt to bring harmony to the ticking of the clock.

Jolene was sprawled on Wren's bed, her head at the foot so that she could see through the open slant of the door in case Kevin came by. Jolene was in love with Kevin. It was his proximity that perpetuated this crush, which had lasted since second grade when she had become Wren's closest friend. Now the angular presence of a man, especially a sixteen-year-old one, sent Jolene into a fluctuating state of chills and flushes matched only by her recent hankering for Mr. Kensley, the new minister at the church, who had become as enticing by his distance as Kevin was by his proximity.

Wren shut the door.

"Wren Jackson," Jolene said huffily. She was miffed by her friend's apparent lack of interest in her love life.

"He's not even home, Jolene," Wren said, putting a record on the turntable and setting the needle. "Maybe you should be spending the afternoon at Melanie Washburn's." The melancholy notes of "Brian's Song" drifted into the room.

"Oh, that's so sad!" Jolene moaned, clutching a pillow to her chest. "It's so tragic!"

"I'll play something else," Wren said.

"Oh no, leave it. I love it. It's just the way I feel. Lonely, rejected, unloved. I'm truly unloved, Wren. I'm not just saying that for sympathy."

"Having a boyfriend isn't everything," Wren said. She sat down on the floor, her back against her laundry hamper.

"That's great for you to say. You've got Sam Holland," Jolene pouted. She flung herself over so that she was staring at the ceiling, the pillow still pressed to her chest.

"I don't have him exactly," Wren protested.

"Well, I don't know what you'd call it. He's phoned you about ten times in two weeks, and he invited you to the movies last weekend. That counts, even though you couldn't go. I mean, he's invited you somewhere two weekends in a row." Jolene flung the pillow aside and shook her fists at the ceiling. "And here I am, pining away. I swear to you, Wren, if Barney Fife asked me out, I'd go. That's how bad it is."

"I thought you were waiting for Kevin."

"Talk about lost causes." Jolene sighed and turned over on her elbow so that she was looking down at Wren. "It's like waiting to be discovered, like Jane Eyre and Mr. Rochester. I always thought one night I'd be sitting downstairs at the dining-room table, candlelight between us, and Kevin would look up from his fried chicken and say, 'Oh, Jolene, you're just the girl I've been looking for. Think of all the years we've wasted, all the days, all the nights.'

"But now Melanie Washburn's sitting next to him and I'm talking to your granddaddy all through dinner. I think I should give up." Jolene pulled one of Wren's stuffed animals into her arms and cuddled it.

"Of course there's Mr. Kensley." Jolene's face lit up, eyes flashing a picture of the blond minister in his black robe, the Bible to his chest, his wrist curved around it so that his watch showed. It was a digital watch with a black empty face until he pressed the button and the time flashed blue on its surface. The watch seemed to denote a hidden person. Beneath his robe Mr. Kensley could have on jeans and a T-shirt that said *No Nukes* for all they knew. He could be wearing suspenders or a heavy leather belt with *Honda* on its brass buckle. He had a motorcycle. Wren and Jolene had seen him on it, his face hidden behind the polarized visor of his red helmet. He had been wearing fatigue boots with metal toes and a slick blue jacket that billowed behind him in the wind.

"Mr. Kensley has a wife," Wren said solemnly.

"Of course he does," Jolene said.

"Then what's the point in liking him?"

"I don't want to marry him, for heaven's sake, Wren!" Jolene sat up and crossed her legs. Her curly hair bounced emphatically. "I just want to think about him. Talk to him sometimes. Find out what he's really like."

"I don't think he'll tell you."

"Then I'll imagine something. That's better anyway."

They could hear the front door open and close.

"That's him!" Jolene whispered. "I know it is. Open the door, Wren!" She lounged back against the headboard while Wren opened the door and looked over the banister.

"Is he coming?" Jolene whispered, already impatient with holding her pose. "Is he?"

Kevin took the stairs two at the time. "Wren!"

"In here," Wren called back, watching Jolene, who was looking as seductive as she could.

"Tell Grandmother I've gone to play tennis with Melanie," he said in the doorway and was on his way to his room to change.

"He didn't even see me!" Jolene wailed softly.

"Jolene," Wren said, shutting the door resolutely, "he's seen you before."

Kevin left his damp tennis gear in the mudroom beside his grandmother's gardening clothes and came into the kitchen where she was at the table hulling strawberries. Her paring knife slipped under the tight green stem and lifted out the hull, then quartered the berry in two swift strokes. Bliss dropped the quarters in a glass bowl.

"Aren't these beautiful?" she asked while Kevin took one of the glistening berries and popped it in his mouth, catching the hull with his teeth. "Mr. Keefer came by with them just a little while ago and they were so pretty and fresh I thought we'd have them for dessert tonight."

Kevin took another and sat down across from her. He looked frazzled, his hair touseled with damp curls, skin still flushed from his tennis game.

"You took Melanie home?" Bliss asked.

"Yeah. Her family's going out for dinner tonight and she had to get changed."

"Then you're free for a while?" Bliss' knife slipped off a ripe berry and into her finger. "Darn." She went to the sink and ran cold water over the cut, then examined it, pulling the slit apart. A thin line of blood showed.

"Is it bad?" Kevin asked. "Need a bandage?"

"I have one right here." Bliss dried her hand with a paper towel and rummaged in her desk drawer beneath the phone book, store coupons, and dental appointment slips to find a Band-Aid. "Put it on," she said, holding her finger out to him.

Kevin drew her hand to him and pressed the gauze center carefully to the cut, then wrapped the adhesive around. "Okay?"

"Thanks. Now let me get these strawberries finished," Bliss said. "Can we talk while I do it?"

"Sure." Kevin ate another berry and tossed the hull into the colander. "What's up?"

"I had a letter from your mother. It was about her plans for the future. The move to Chicago and so forth. All the things she's already told you." Bliss was watching him. He seemed so relaxed, hardly concerned, although the mention of his mother usually made him tense up, drew the muscles in his arms, worked at his jaw and forehead.

"Kevin," she said, "I've already told Wren this. I told her yesterday, and I want you to know she understands."

"What is it?" Now he was getting anxious. He put his arms tight to his sides like a primitive statue.

It wasn't that Bliss wanted him to panic, not exactly, but she did want him to be prepared. This wasn't like a shot when a relaxed muscle made all the difference. It was more like reacting to a disaster, those incredible acts of courage people performed when necessity provoked them.

"What is it, Grandmother? What did she say?" His fear was building, fists tense on his thighs, toes lifted against the tops of his tennis shoes. His eyebrows darkened, a ridge of foreboding across his forehead.

"She's getting a divorce," Bliss said quietly. "It's a formality, Kevin. That's all it is. She hasn't lived with your dad for a long time, and I don't suppose she sees any future in it."

"That's it?" he asked. "That's what she told you?" His lips were tight. The words cut through them like a knife into muscle. His face was chalky, as if he had bled dry.

"I've got to go out," he said. He was already on his way to the door.

"But it's almost dinner time," Bliss protested, turning to look after him. It was too late to hold out her arms. He was gone.

"Don't be out long, Kevin!" Bliss called after him. She could hear the engine turning over, the screech of brakes when he backed out of the drive, then the squeal of tires as he took off down the quiet Sunday street.

"O Lord." Bliss put her hands to her face. The cut finger throbbed, and she wrapped her other hand around it. "O Lord, don't let him do anything foolish."

She was holding her breath. It occurred to her that she had been holding her breath for months now, dreading whatever would threaten Kevin's fragility. He could wreck the car, not intentionally but foolishly, because his mind was racing beyond the car and his skill was elementary. He could hurt himself. Didn't he know the damage Karen had done was nothing compared to what he could do to himself?

There was no place for him to go. Melanie was on her way out to dinner. There was no old friend to whom he could take his grief, no secret place that would bring him solace. Finally he went to the edge of the river where he could look across to the town, not at his street exactly, but at the tops of familiar buildings, the steeple of the First Baptist Church, the courthouse dome, the fringe of trees along the riverbank. This was where he lived, these empty places, so quiet and solemn in the twilight of Sunday. He put his head against the steering wheel, not wanting to see.

He was so tired. The drive, the anxiety of wondering

where to go and what to do, had exhausted him. He wanted to disappear, to move out of himself, separate mind from heart, escape. After a few minutes, he curled up on the front seat, legs tucked under the steering wheel, his hands over his face as if he believed, like a child might, that hiding his eyes took him out of view.

Huddled on the seat, he began to cry. Nobody was there to hear him, but he knew what the sound was like, the retching sobs that tore out of his chest and shook him relentlessly until he was heaving and sweating on the vinyl.

Night came and the heaving stopped. Slowly the shudders became tiny trembles; the sobs, inaudible murmurings. That was when he felt the loneliness. It came at him with the first night calls of birds from the woods behind him, with the buzz of insects off the slow river and the slight slapping of the water. He waited for it to come, to pierce his skin like stings, to worm into his brain, his quivering stomach, his empty heart.

It's not so bad, he thought, feeling his injury.

He remembered the dread he'd once felt at having a blood sample drawn, the unrealistic fear he'd known, panic far more painful than the jab of the blade into the pushed-up flesh of his index finger could be. But he had not been able to sit there; he had jerked his hand out of the nurse's tight, angry grip time after time until finally Bliss had come and taken him on her lap, her arms as warm as wool on his skin, her breath as calm and patient as his was rattling. She had held him like that while the busy nurse stalked him, waiting for her moment.

In his grandmother's arms, he had known the inevitability of the prick, had traveled in his memory to all the seconds spent on that sensation, so quick and violent and then so harmless. A piece of cotton pressed momentarily on the spot did the trick.

And so he finally put out his finger, felt the sting, saw his blood being pipetted up the tiny tube, pressed the cotton ball tightly on and held it there while his grandmother's arms rocked him as if he were a baby and not eleven years old with knobby legs dangling to the floor, mouth stained with cherry soda, a quarter reward already in his pocket.

He sat up in the car, rubbed his hands over his face and through his matted hair. He started the ignition quickly, before he could think anymore. The sound was like the world breaking open. He clutched the wheel and reversed the car. He went home to Bliss.

Chapter 9

The Hollands were having a pig-pickin'. Sam invited Wren early in the week, before she could have other plans for Saturday afternoon.

"I know you're going to see your dad," he said, sitting on the stool next to her in the drugstore. "I could ride my bike into town after lunch and then we could go out to my house together. Or my brother Paul could come get you. He's home from college for the summer."

"Or Kevin could bring me out," Wren said. She fingered the straw in her cup, then mashed it flat.

"Then you'll come?"

"Yes, I'd like to." Wren poked at the ice in her cup with the mangled straw. "I wanted to go to the movies last weekend, Sam, but Grandmother had invited people for dinner and she expected me to be there."

"I know that's what you told me." Sam looked at her in the mirror. There was a slight distortion in her face, a tired, preoccupied look. "But I wasn't sure if I should believe it. I know going to the movies is more like a date than going to the Reed Farm was. I thought your grand-parents might not let you go out with me when we'd be alone, even though we'd be walking. You understood that, didn't you? Dad would bring me into town and then pick me up later."

"It was the dinner, Sam. I promise." Wren smiled, but her smile was wan and more polite than persuasive.

"What is it, Wren?" Sam lay his hand over hers. His fingers were cold and damp from his cup, and they sent a slight chill up her arm.

"Oh, I don't know. Just a family thing really." Wren caught his fingers between hers and pulled his hand closer, warming it, although Ginny was watching from her side of the counter. "We just found out Mother's divorcing Daddy. Grandmother says it's just a formality, and I guess she's right. I know it doesn't really change anything, at least not right away. But it hurts all the same."

"We'll have a good day Saturday," Sam said because he knew there was nothing he could say about her parents that could matter. "Paul's home and my married sister Kate will be here with her children and my sister Lisa and a lot of neighbors—farm people, but you probably know most of them."

"I may not fit in," Wren said, releasing his fingers. Maybe he expected too much of her.

"My mom's gonna love you," Sam said. He put his fingers on her neck and ran his thumb up under her hair. It was such an open gesture and almost convincing.

Wren shivered. Were there mothers like that, women other than Bliss who could spin magic, drawing children in to treasure them, protect them, help them love themselves? She wanted to believe there were. She knew there would be if wishing could make it so.

Chapter Nine

Kathryn Holland was big. She opened her arms as if she could gather the sheaves in all at once, draw the world to her heavy bosom and hold it safe. Now she put her arms around this little thing Sam had brought home with him, her face hot and blotched from the bike ride from town. There was nothing hearty about this child although she had a good face, lightly freckled beneath a slow tan, blue eyes hooded by a thick fringes of lashes; woeful eyes Kathryn would call them until she saw Wren smile and the eyes lit up, unshadowed, as if the sun had suddenly appeared from behind a cloud.

"So you're Wren," she said, holding the girl back to look at her.

Wren's smile was hesitant but worth the wait.

"You're Bliss and Bill Jackson's granddaughter. Tom's child. I was in high school with Tom. Did you know that, Sam? Wren's dad was quite a card, always clever and witty. Everybody liked him. We bought our first insurance policy from him." She squeezed Wren's shoulder. "Is he getting better?" she asked softly. "I know it's hard on him, but I reckon it's about as hard on you."

"He's better," Wren said. "Much better." He would never be the man Mrs. Holland remembered, but at least he recognized his daughter and cared that she had come that morning. Those little things counted to Wren. It was hard to explain how much they mattered, how important a smile became, a certain tone of voice, the grip of fingers against her own.

Kathryn Holland let her go and then Sam was taking her arm. From one safety to another, as quickly and easily as that.

"We're going to wash up. Wren even brought another shirt to put on after the bike ride," Sam said. "Then we'll help you, Mom."

"Yes, Mrs. Holland. I'd like to help."

"You'll get your chance." Kathryn laughed. "Everybody here does. You rest a little while. There's not much to do yet. And Wren, call me Kathryn. Everybody does, even my grandbabies, although heaven knows, I sure wanted to be Grandma bad enough."

The house was the big old farmhouse John Holland had been born in gradually remodeled, modernized, and added to. Still the kitchen had oak floors and some of the walls and ceilings were narrow boards, their seams disappearing under numerous coats of paint. The furniture was a mixture of family heirlooms and Sears, and there was a shabby, lived-in quality about the rooms, as if Kathryn Holland were less concerned about beauty than she was about function. The house was comfortable and a little messy, as though someone had stopped midway through spring cleaning— windows sparkled but a fine layer of dust clung to the surfaces of fine old wood and the morning paper was in crumpled sections and flung on top of a years' worth of magazines on the living-room floor.

Wren washed up in the new bathroom off the kitchen and changed her shirt while she listened to Sam at the kitchen sink where he splashed water and yelled out the window to his sister, who had just arrived with her family. She heard the back door slam and the room fill up with noise, children squealing and laughing as they went after Sam. Then Kate's voice, rich and relaxed, as if she could let the antics around her go unheeded while she embraced and spoke with her brother.

Wren stood in the bathroom, wondering how she'd make her entrance. She knew there was no reason she couldn't simply open the door and step out, her hand reaching for Kate's and the proper words crossing her lips as effortlessly as they did with Bliss or Kathryn Holland or even her mother. Each of those women had their own special kind of grace: Bliss' was athletic but charming; Kathryn's, warm and abundant; Karen's, stylish and clever. They were so different, and yet they knew the power of the well-placed word, the easy, comfortable phrases that lent themselves to equally appropriate responses.

When would Wren learn those words? At some special age, on a particular birthday, did those phrases push beyond a meaningless "have a nice day" to the more valuable subtleties of breeding? Wren wanted them now, this minute when she was stranded in a bathroom while around her a family wove their own special web of private humor and shared moments. She was isolated at their center, as solitary and motionless as the space within a vortex.

She felt so lonely, even alien, like a visitor in a strange land where the language was uncomprehensible and the customs, engimas. She couldn't do it. No amount of courage could force her out of the closed, protected space of the bathroom, and so she stood there like a prisoner, locked in her inability to imagine herself anywhere else.

"Wren!" Sam was at the door. "Wren, hurry up. Kate's here. Come on, the kids want to meet my girl." They waited, she on her side of the door, he on his.

She put out her hand, turning the cool knob so that the lock clicked open, but she didn't have the strength for the quick tug the door required.

"Wren?" A softer sound, expectant and welcoming.

She pulled at the metal, opening the door, taking the necessary step backward when what she wanted to do, what suddenly seemed right, was to come forward. Sam was grinning at her, an identical two-year-old dangling from each arm.

"Here she is!" he announced, pushing a giggling red-headed baby at her. "And here they are. That's Katrina you've got," he said. "And this one"—nodding at the child he held—"is Kathryn."

The baby in her arms clutched Wren around the neck and wrapped her chubby legs around her waist.

"And this is Kate," Sam said, turning toward his sister, a young woman in jeans who was wiping the face of a four-year-old boy who had obviously just finished a Popsicle. "And Kris."

"Would you believe their daddy's name doesn't start with a *K*," Kate said, dropping her cloth in the sink and coming to meet Wren. "His name is Greg and he's out there telling Paul how to cook the pig. Nothing is more boring than men outdoing each other with their cooking techniques. I've never understood how they could complain about women's conversations." She put out her hand and touched Wren's free shoulder. "I'm so glad you could come. There's no better way to get to know the Hollands than en masse. One at a time we don't have anything like the same effect."

Katrina dug her head into Wren's shoulder and shut her eyes.

"I think they'll take a nap," Kate said, brushing her hand gently up the baby's back, "if we can find a quiet place."

"My room," Sam suggested. "I'll put some blankets on the floor." He gave Kathryn to her mother.

"Shall I take that one?" Kate asked Wren. "I'm used to juggling two."

"Oh no, I like holding her. Maybe I could rock her to sleep." Wren touched the soft red hair, and it lifted against her palm.

"Well, help yourself. There's a rocking chair." Kate cradled the other sleepy child because she knew how to rock standing up.

Wren settled in the chair, pulling the baby to her chest, her short legs in her lap.

When Sam came down he found them there: Wren in the rocker with the sleeping child; Kate walking to and fro, humming softly into the head resting on her breast; Kris drowsy on the sofa, his thumb in his mouth. From where Sam stood, it seemed that Wren was at their center, as content and relaxed as he had hoped she'd be.

Wren looked up then and saw him watching her. She closed her eyes, feeling his eyes, the endearing, foolish grin he couldn't control, and felt pass between them the sure and precious knowledge that she had been taken in.

Paul Holland, as tall and lanky as his dad and brother, was spreading coals in the bottom of the cooker with a shovel. "You must be Wren," he said, latching the firedoor shut. "Wanta peek?"

He lifted the hinged lid they had fashioned after cutting a five-hundred-gallon oil drum crosswise. The pig had been split down the backbone so that it lay flat on the grid. The smell of hickory smoke wafted into Wren's face on the heat.

"That's it," Paul said, lowering the lid. "We don't look very often or for very long because every time the lid goes up, the temperature comes down."

"How long does it take?" Wren asked, putting her fingers on the lid. Heat popped into her hand.

"A pig this size takes all day, so we'll probably start eating about six. Four o'clock is where you come in." His eyes were laughing just the way his mother's did.

"Me?" Wren backed into Sam, who took her arms and pulled her closer to his chest.

"That's when we start mopping," Sam said. "Mom has the sauce on the stove right now. When the pig's almost done, we turn it over and start putting barbecue sauce on it with old-fashioned dish mops. You get to mop."

"Mom's in charge of that," Paul said, "and she always gets as many volunteers as she can muster. She'll also get you in the kitchen making cornbread."

"You might just find yourself in there with her." Kathryn Holland dropped her hand on the cooker and held it there a few seconds, testing the heat. "Why, this pig wouldn't be anything without cornbread," she said. "You might as well have turkey without dressing or beer without peanuts."

"Speaking of beer, where's that cooler?" Paul wanted to know.

"I hid it," Kathryn said. "I can promise you one thing, it's safe and you're sober, at least until you finish this pig."

"One beer, Ma." Paul grinned as he sidled up to his mother and put his arm around her. "One, Ma. I've been working all day." He smacked at her cheek.

"Just look at him," Kathryn said. "Comes in here from college two days ago, stuffs that junk back into his room—at least what he doesn't leave in the hall for us to stumble over—and goes off to see his buddies without a word. No kiss, no loving, no 'Hey, Mom, how you been.' And now here he comes smooching after me for a beer. A beer, mind you!" She hugged him to her and kissed him firmly on the cheek. "It's in the barn, and don't you tell a soul."

"Watch the pig, you two!" Paul was on his way to the barn.

"Well, I'm going to look at the sauce and see about Kate and the babies," Kathryn said. "You children stay around now so I can find you when I need you." She was off to the house, her flip-flops slapping the grass.

"Well?" Sam said, his arms still holding Wren close. He lowered his face to her neck so she could feel his breath behind her ear, although she was watching Kathryn Holland disappear into the house.

No wonder Sam was so sure of himself. How could he miss with a mother like her? There seemed to be so little held back, nothing like the reserve Wren felt separating herself from Karen. She could feel Sam's breath in the curls that fell around her ear.

"Do you know how lucky you are?" she asked, putting her hands on his bare arms so that she was holding on to him, too.

"Sometimes I guess I don't," Sam said, his lips hovering at her neck for a moment before she felt a soft brush as he lay a kiss there. "But today I do."

It was after ten when Paul dropped Sam and Wren off in front of her house. Sam lifted her bike off the bed of the truck and walked it into the yard.

"I've got an errand downtown," Paul said through the open window. "I'll pick you up in twenty minutes, little brother."

The truck moved out of the drive, and the lawn was suddenly shadowed with lamplight falling from the living-room windows onto the crimson blooms of Bliss' azaleas.

"I'd better tell Grandmother we're here," Wren said and slipped into the house. She was back in a moment, shutting the door softly behind her. "I told her we'd be out here on the stoop," she said, "unless you want to go in."

"I guess I'd better be out here when Paul gets back," Sam said, sitting down on the step.

"An errand at ten-thirty." Wren giggled, settling beside him.

"Well, he tried," Sam laughed, although he could hear nervousness in both their voices. He felt himself turning shy, sinking into himself and away from the responsibility he knew he had of making the rest of their time together go well. "I had a good time," he said finally.

"That's my line," Wren said, a laugh popping awkwardly into her voice.

"I did have a great time, Wren." He put his arm across her shoulder without any subtle stretching or prolonged yawn. If he were going to take a risk, he might as well get on with it.

"So did I—have a great time," Wren said. "Your family's nice. I really like your mother."

"I thought you might think she comes on a little strong.

98

I mean, everybody in our family just says what they think in the simplest possible way." Sam felt her shoulder pressing toward him. "I know she liked you, and even if she didn't, I'd still be right here."

"That's what you call saying something the simplest way?" Wren asked.

"Actually, I think there's a better one." Sam's mouth brushed across her cheek, lingering while he waited for her to turn her face toward his.

She didn't.

"Wren," he whispered into her hair, "I've only kissed three girls in my whole life and two of them were playing a stupid game at a Christmas party. The third one wasn't much better. Meg James. It was after a J.V. basketball game and—"

"Sh-h-h," Wren said and turned her mouth to his.

Chapter 10

 In a few minutes, Wren would be playing the processional for the eighth-grade graduation ceremony at Larkwood Elementary School. She sat on the leather seat before the old grand piano on the edge of the stage, her face tucked in, eyes to the yellow splintery keys, hands flat on her thighs, their moisture absorbing into the soft folds of her dress.

Karen had offered to buy her an outfit, consolation prize from a mother who couldn't come herself. "I'll send you money for a new dress," she'd said. "Something soft and pretty with a lace collar and cuffs or those lovely little puffed sleeves the girls are wearing." She sounded like an advertisement. "Wear those dainty little things while you can, sweetheart, while you have such slender, tanned arms."

"I've already bought a dress," Wren said into the receiver. She held her mouth close, almost whispering. She didn't want Bliss to know what her mother was offering.

"Oh, well," Karen said lightly, "then I'll send you something else. What would you like? More beads for your necklace. A watch? Certainly something you can keep. I know—a ring, a birthstone. A ruby set in gold filigree to show it off. Something delicate.. How about that?" Her voice floated uncontained by the wires and the mechanism of the earpiece. Everybody in the world could hear.

"That would be nice, Mother," Wren said.

"I wish I could be there, you know that, don't you, Wren? If it weren't for this meeting the next morning."

"I understand," Wren said. "It's no big deal."

"Why, of course it is. Your last day in the school you've been attending all your life. Ready to go to high school. You're growing up, Wren."

"When can you come, Mother?"

"The middle of June, I hope. At least by the end of the month. I'll stay several days, I promise. I'll make this up to you, Wren. We'll have a wonderful time."

So no matter how much she wanted to be, Karen wasn't in the audience that waited impatiently on the squeaky folding chairs in the warm gymnasium. She wasn't whispering softly to the mother in front of her, leaning forward from her seat to share the excitement of this moment. She didn't even know the other mothers, much less the students in Wren's class.

They would be odd faces to her, new suits to be grown into, pastel dresses to be worn every Sunday all summer. She wouldn't see the years in their faces, had little memory of their chubby eagerness in kindergarten, their thin awkwardness in fourth grade, their sixth-grade belligerence, their chronic bursts of laughter in the eighth. Tonight ended something and even though the high school was only two miles away, as familiar as older siblings, ballgames and beauty pageants could make it, it was still an incomprehensible country, threatening them with weighty textbooks, austere locker-lined hallways, and bells that clanged out directions.

Wren looked up to see her class waiting in the hall outside the gym, fidgeting in their new clothes. Mrs. Dudley nodded to her from behind the curtain on the other end of the stage, and Wren brought her hands to the keys, focused for a moment on the first line of the music and then struck the opening chords of *Pomp and Circumstance.*

Her classmates began their solemn march to the reserved seats in front of the stage. They passed grandparents and parents, faculty, siblings, aunts and uncles, friends from other classes. They looked straight ahead, at Wren in fact, afraid that they might spot a familiar face along the aisle and grin involuntarily.

Because Wren knew the music, her fingers found the keys unhesitatingly and so she looked out at the slow procession, the students filing into their seats by rehearsed arrangement, the class officers stepping out of line to come up on the stage where they would make brief, practiced speeches of welcome and appreciation.

The faces of her friends held so taut and solemn seemed strange to her. It was the distance, she thought, suddenly wishing she hadn't agreed to provide the music. She wished she were among them now, securely among the J's where she'd been all these years.

She looked back at her music. Notes split from whole to half, from quarters to eighths. The bass clef disintegrated, but she didn't need the notes. She reached for the final chord and struck. Hands folded once more, she looked out at her class. She didn't recognize a soul.

"We'll all go out to dinner," Bliss said. "You and Sam. Kevin and Melanie. Bill and me. That is, if you can put up with old folks for an evening."

"Oh, Grandmother, where can we go?"

"I thought you'd like the Candlelight Inn, either there or the country club. Someplace especially nice for your graduation party. What do you think?"

"The Candlelight Inn," Wren said.

She could only faintly remember the restaurant's dark paneling with its dimly lit sconces, the candles and flowers on the pale blue cloths, for years had passed since she and Kevin had gone there with Karen. But she knew it had been a good night, its colors captured in her memory.

She remembered that Karen and Kevin had danced, Karen urging him around the small dance floor while Kevin, who was probably ten at the time, held himself as straight and unyielding as he could, looking nervously toward the table's shadowed safety. Wren had danced, too, but not with Kevin. Karen had pulled her onto the floor and they had danced together, holding hands and swirling their loose skirts in a soft sway with the music. Wren had felt herself floating. It seemed only Karen's hands kept her earthbound, although she had believed as she looked up at her mother's beautiful face that Karen could fly if she wanted to. They could both fly.

"We can dance there," Wren said. Now she was thinking of Sam and how wonderful he had looked at the school dances. He'd had a flow she could imagine moving with. There was no reason Sam couldn't fly, too.

"Sam and I can dance there," she said.

"Then invite him for tomorrow night," Bliss said. And Wren did.

They sat at a round corner table, candlelight licking the frosted glass chimney in the center. Sam wore his khaki suit and Wren her graduation dress and the ring Karen had sent. Wren put her hand over the ring in her lap, feeling it scratch on her palm. It was beautiful but more expensive than any gift her friends had received, and it felt heavy and unnatural on her finger. She'd rather think about the book Sam had given her wrapped in crisp pink paper and a silver ribbon.

The book was *Sonnets from the Portuguese* bound in blue cloth with gold lettering. She had held the poems in her lap while Sam stood stiffly by, looking down at the volume as though he couldn't bring himself to look at her. She couldn't look at him either, and so she turned the pages slowly, feeling the weight of the heavy paper between her fingers and catching a word here and there.

She had heard of Elizabeth Barrett and her poet husband. She knew how Robert Browning had rescued the sickly woman from her bed, drawing her out into the world she'd never seen except from the narrow panes of her bedroom window. She remembered how they had loved each other and had put words to it.

So the book in her hands amazed her. How had he thought of such a gift, so perfectly personal that simply holding it astounded her. She could only think that he hadn't read the words so delicately formed and arranged on exquisite spaces of blank paper, and so didn't understand what a gift like this might mean to her.

"I hope you like it," she heard him saying. His voice was

almost a whisper. "It's Mom's favorite book of poems, and so I thought you might like it, too."

"I do," she whispered, still unable to look at him. "I can't believe how beautiful it is."

"Good," Sam breathed. "I was sort of worried about it."

Now she could look up at him. In fact, she got up and pressed the book to her chest. "It's a wonderful present. I just wish it were your graduation so I could give you something, too."

"And what would you give me?" Sam laughed. Their awkwardness had dissolved into relief.

"I don't know," Wren said. "But something terrific like this. Something special that you could always keep, like I'll always keep this book."

So now in the restaurant, they were giving each other a memory to keep. Side by side at the table, they felt themselves divided into couples: Bill and Bliss as comfortable as years can make two people, Kevin and Melanie alternately giggling and acting sophisticated. Sam and Wren were the most subdued, for the evening's spell seemed woven just for them—the rich food served with skillful elegance, the small glasses of champagne they were allowed, the band playing softly behind them. The night belonged to them.

On the dance floor, Wren put her hand on Sam's shoulder and felt the pressure of his fingers at her back, so light and sure they startled her. Their hands locked, and she looked up at him, the angle of face that exposed the jaw, half a nose, an eye almost closed.

"Sam," she said softly to make him look at her, "what do you think will happen to us?"

He stopped moving and held her still. "I haven't the slightest idea. Anyway, wouldn't we rather be surprised?"

"I don't like surprises," Wren said. "They scare me."

"Then I'll tell you," Sam said. He drew her closer so that her cheek was pressed into his jacket. She could feel his heartbeat. "After the summer is over, we'll go to school together. Then, before you know it, we'll graduate and go to college, the same college. In fact, you have to skip a grade so we can go to college at the same time. Then we'll get married, either before or during or after. And then we'll get jobs that make us a lot of money so that on vacations we can take fantastic trips and eat in restaurants like this every week and have foster children in addition to our own. Several children, lots of children." He was laughing.

She could hear the laughter, a soft gurgle at her ear before it broke and spilled over her light head. She knew he could see all that. She had heard the realness of it in his voice. And so, nestled against his chest and keeping time with him, she believed it too.

Chapter 11

Kevin went to see his father. It was two days after Wren's graduation, and he went alone. He knew his dad was better and had begun to talk, making the kind of stilted conversation available to him when his world was inside one room and nothing ever happened except that he had treatments, took medicine, and saw a psychiatrist. There was little concern for existence elsewhere, no interest in the news, no worries that weren't petty, selfish ones. He knew his dad would be wrapped up in himself, a cocoon of antidepressants surrounding him as warmly as if he were a larva. Every year or two, Tom Jackson was reborn.

"Hello, Dad," Kevin said from the doorway.

Tom was dressed and sat by the window in an easy chair. The window was open but blocked by a heavy metal grid.

"Son." Tom made no gesture toward him but his voice was strong. His tongue didn't twist thickly as it once had, pushing out misarranged sounds and eliminating letters altogether in an exhausted slur.

"How are you, Dad?" Kevin came into the room that because of the opened window didn't smell as medicinal as he remembered. There was a lightness in the air, like an after-shave scent.

"Better, I hope." Tom put out his hand.

Kevin took it, but then pulled back as soon as he could. Touching was dangerous. It meant there was a connection between them. If they embraced, he would suddenly be Tom Jackson's little boy again, and he couldn't afford to be a child.

"The medicine is helping you then," Kevin said. He sat on the edge of the bed. It was too high to sit on comfortably.

"The shock treatments are," Tom said and saw Kevin grimace. It was a familiar frown, that spontaneous wrinkle that narrowed his son's eyes and forehead and made him look hostile, as if he were hearing inner rumblings that could explode on his face.

Tom remembered that look from years ago when Kevin poured over his first readers, screwing up his face to recall a word for which no phonetic sound seemed just right. Tom was faintly surprised that he could remember. Those were the kinds of things the electroshock treatments caused him to forget—little blocks of time, a minute scene that had been at the time wonderfully intense with emotion.

Of course, sometimes he couldn't remember big things, or current ones. Once he'd forgotten where Karen lived. But that didn't bother him as much as the lost moments with the children, which seemed to him infinitely more precious because they proved so undependable.

"The treatments aren't so bad," he said now to Kevin, who was looking at the flowers Bliss had brought on

Saturday instead of toward his father. "I suppose hearing it described—120 volts of electricity into your head—makes it sound terrible, and I would have been afraid that first time if I'd been able to feel anything. Sometimes it's a relief just to feel. But I don't dread them very much now. I go to sleep and I wake up. Maybe a little nausea. That's all."

Tom felt strange talking about it, though. His life in the hospital didn't seem specific enough to talk about. It seemed so pale and dreamlike now that Kevin was with him wearing bright clothes and looking solid and contained. He had on a yellow knit shirt, chinos, and loafers; he looked like Tom had looked twenty years ago, only tighter, more tensely strung.

"Tell me about you," Tom said finally.

"There's nothing to tell," Kevin replied, head bent to the lavender iris Bliss had brought.

He was closed up. Coming down the hall to this room, he'd let himself fall away so that when he pushed open the door and saw his father, he could zip up his empty self like putting a jacket on a scarecrow. He didn't want to feel anything except detachment, as if he were dropping in on a stranger. Still the room held familiarity for him. Its barren, dismal interior was like the shell inside his head. He could furnish it with worn, uncomfortable furniture, springs and batting bulging like dark thoughts. His head was tumescent, weighted with his vision of this hidden living place, a crawl space behind his eyes. Where did he live, anyway?

Kevin focused above the curling, furry blooms of the iris to see his grandparents' house, but the colors didn't seem right to him. The bricks had turned black as if a shadow had fallen over them, the windows were murky and dusty with webs, the shrubs and grass withered brown. Where did he live?

Hadn't there been a bright place once, white eyelet curtains blowing, paisley pillows on the soft chairs, polished brass catching light? Hadn't he once lived in a place like that?

"When are you coming home, Dad?" he asked, turning to Tom. Was this man real? Was he the only true, unchanging fact in Kevin's life? Was depression, insanity, the only kind of stability he could depend on? That and Karen's absence?

"A few more weeks, I guess," Tom said. His voice was fading. The visit was such an effort for him, and he felt so tired now. He wanted to tell Kevin how tired he felt, but he was afraid to.

"School's out tomorrow. I guess you know that. Wren graduated from the eighth grade last Friday night. Mother couldn't come, but she'll be coming for a visit soon. I guess Grandmother told you that."

Tom felt helplessness sliding between his ribs. It assaulted his throat and lungs, forcing him to take shallow, empty breaths. He didn't want to hear anything about home. Sometimes he thought everything he heard was old news, events played out over and over again while he was still feeling the original pain of them so acutely.

"So maybe she'll be here when you come home. She promised to stay a few days before she moves to Chicago."

Tom felt his heart break under the weight of what he couldn't bear to hear.

"I guess we shouldn't have been surprised, about the

divorce, I mean," Kevin said easily, as if he didn't see his father's expression, the animal fear crossing his eyes, the dry sucking mouth opening for a silent howl. "Grandmother made it sound so inevitable, you know, like it wasn't anybody's fault. It's not going to really change anything. It's just something that was bound to happen. That's how we've got to think about it."

Now he saw. The body wrenched forward, arms limp and useless, head flung back like a convulsion.

"Dad!" He was holding the body. Trembles like electric shocks traveled between them, searing them together. "You didn't know?" he cried into the lolling face. "Grandmother hadn't told you?" He cradled the head and shoulders to his pounding chest. "It's all right, Daddy," he said. "You're all right." His arms grew weak, all his strength pouring out to support his parent.

"I didn't mean to hurt you, Daddy," he sobbed. But even while he cradled the man in his arms, he wasn't sure.

Kevin brought home a *D* in chemistry. He folded the computer slip into his jeans pocket along with the *C*'s in English, Algebra, and German, before he got into the station wagon beside Melanie. It was eleven o'clock in the morning, and they sat in the parking lot with the sun low in their faces. There was a chilly bite in the air after a soaking rain the night before, but the car was hot and uncomfortable, having been closed up while they attended the final day of school.

Melanie was sneezing. She hunched over, a tissue crammed to her nose, and expelled a series of quick, wet spasms.

"I wish you'd take something," Kevin said, starting the car.

"I do take something," Melanie said, hunting for another dry tissue in her bag. "It'll be over in a few weeks."

"What will? The opening movement of the sneeze chorus?" Kevin gunned the car out of the school lot.

"No, the allergy season." Melanie sniffed and leaned her head back on the seat. "Anyway, it's me who's enduring it, not you."

"I listen to you, don't I? I contribute my handkerchief when the Kleenex give out."

"Well, you needn't." Melanie dabbed at her eyes which were still tearing. "You can put me out at home."

"I thought your baby-sitting job didn't start until Monday."

"It doesn't."

"Then let's go hit a few tennis balls. I've got a game at the club this afternoon and I could use a warm-up."

"You'll fuss at me," Melanie said. "I know you will. You're in a lousy mood, Kevin."

"Well, it helps if you return a ball now and then. I mean, that's the point of the game."

"See. Just listen to you already." Melanie sneezed. "I want to go home, Kevin."

"What about tonight?" he asked, forcing himself to sound contrite as he took a corner in the direction of her house.

"What about it?"

"I thought you'd come watch me play, then we could go for a swim, get a burger somewhere. Then go out to the river."

"All planned, huh?"

"It's what I thought you'd want, too." Kevin pulled up in front of her house.

"It is, Kevin." She put her hand on his thigh, and he dropped his hand on top of hers. "What's wrong with you? We were fine at Wren's party. I thought we were okay together. I mean, I felt comfortable with you and your family. I thought we cared about each other."

"I do care about you, Melanie. I just hate your hay fever." He grinned.

"It's almost June. I promise you a clear head in June." She leaned over to kiss his cheek.

"I'll see you after tennis. Can you get a ride to the club?"

"I'll be there." She slipped out of the car and ran up the walk.

Kevin watched her flight and then her disappearing act at the front door because it seemed to him she simply vanished. He couldn't hear the solid thud of the door closing or her racing steps on the stairs as she went to her room, which faced front, where she held back the curtain to see him sitting there as if he expected her to return. What was he waiting for? What did he want?

Looking down at him, she felt a dreadful fear creeping in her head, infectious as it invaded her good thoughts, her summer plans, the anticipation she'd felt just an hour ago when she'd run down the school walk for the last time until fall. Sometimes she truly believed his moodiness was catching, like a germ that traveled by touch, spread by hand and mouth until it deadened the brain to the possibilities of being sixteen and having the summer before them. But she wouldn't let that happen. She would protect them both, even if that meant saving Kevin from himself. She could find a way to do it.

He was pulling away.

"I don't intend to lose you, Kevin Jackson," she said aloud and pressed her cheek to the glass to catch a final glimpse of the orange car. But he had disappeared.

Wren and Jolene were in the stands with Jolene's sisters, who together looked like Pat Boone's girls, all pressed and fresh, although the sun was broiling hot at three o'clock and the air close and breathless. Melanie went to sit with them, her swimsuit and towel in a canvas bag with her makeup. She didn't know why she bothered with makeup. Her watery eyes made mascara a disaster, and she would probably either eat or kiss off however much lipstick she put on.

That was one of the good things about going steady. Getting ready didn't take nearly as much time as it once had, since practically everything done was going to get undone before the evening was over.

She smiled a little to herself, watching Kevin on the court. He looked so good, already deeply tanned, as if summer had come early for him. And his whites sparkled. They were new, selected by her with Bliss' credit card in Kevin's pocket. They had bought the best, checking strength of seams and flexibility of fabric rather than price tags. So he looked good along with playing well, his body like a spring, weight shifting easily, a comfortable, balanced crouch. He looked natural, as if he hadn't had to learn this game and hadn't practiced in all seasons, but had been born to it, Bliss' prowess in his genes, Karen's grace.

Wren thought he was playing too hard. He seemed to be coming into the ball too much, unwilling to wait. She knew he lost power that way, when he let himself get trapped into a running game. But it wasn't his opponent who forced him. John Weaver wasn't nearly the player Kevin was and although their score would appear on the club board, the match wasn't a contest, just a friendly game. So why was Kevin playing so hard, taking victory with such a spread that power seemed unnecessary anymore? He could win with lobs.

Still he raced on, rushing the net foolishly, his running forehand giving up accuracy for impetuous lunges. He was sweating. A wet oval formed down the back of his shirt, his hair curled wetly around his sweatband. He rubbed his hand on his pants, leaving a faint gray streak on the white.

"I wish he'd relax," Wren said to Melanie. "He doesn't have to play this hard."

Jolene adjusted her sun visor and glanced at Melanie. "He's just intense, that's all," she said. "I like intensity in men, don't you?"

"Not especially," Melanie answered, watching the ball sink into the net. "He was keyed up this morning," she said to Wren quietly. "I don't know what's wrong with him, but something is."

"I know he went to see Dad," Wren said. "When he came home, he went straight to his room and stayed there all afternoon. He wouldn't even tell me how Dad was, and I don't think Grandmother knows he went at all. He's so moody lately we all just stay clear of him."

"Well, I think he's perfect in every way," Jolene said.

Melanie and Jolene eyed each other across Wren for a

second, so they didn't see Kevin fall but they heard the skidding screech of sneakers, the thud of racket on asphalt, and then the gasp as Jolene's sisters rose in unison. Maybe they heard the crack, too. At least they knew it was there the second they focused on the body, face down, trembling brown legs extended, the right arm under him, caught between his chest and the hard black surface. He was on his knees, white back curved to the sun, head bent as if he were retching; then slow movement brought him upright because his left hand clutched his right wrist to his chest and left him balanceless. John Weaver was lifting him up. Wren and Melanie dashed onto the court, Jolene in tow.

"Are you all right, Kevin?" John was asking.

Kevin ignored him. "My wrist," he said to Wren and Melanie while Jolene stood between them looking solicitous and grief-stricken. "It's broken." His skin was ashen. Chilling sweat dripped down his neck and pooled at the collar of his shirt.

"I'll get the car," Melanie said. "Wren, get him to sit down."

"I'll help you," Jolene said. "Oh, Kevin, you were playing so great!"

"Well, that's the last you'll see of it this summer, maybe forever." Kevin was shivering as he went slowly out the gate toward the parking lot.

"You should sit," Wren said, holding on to his left side. "If it's broken, you may be in shock."

"I know it's broken, Wren. I just want to get out of here."

Melanie pulled the station wagon up to them.

Chapter Eleven

"I'll go with him," Wren said to Jolene. "See you later."

Jolene frowned because she'd expected to go to the hospital, but she didn't have the courage to ask. "Call me when you know something. Call me from the hospital. Kevin, I feel so bad. I really do."

The car pulled away, leaving Jolene standing at the edge of the parking lot. She watched the car go and already was thinking how he'd look in a cast, what she'd write on it, how at first he wouldn't be able to use his fingers. She would tie his shoes, cut his meat, button his shirts. She would be there every day, just in case he needed her. The fantasy was as blinding as the sun, as heady as Christmas punch, as impossible as any midnight dream.

They brought him home in a cast that enclosed his fingers almost to the knuckles, wrapped around his thumb, and then extended almost to his elbow.

"A fracture," he said to Bliss, who settled him on the family-room sofa with pillows beneath his head and an afghan thrown over his legs. He looked too exposed in his tennis garb, his skin suddenly pale as if he'd lost blood. He was just tired, she knew, and hurting a little because he took the pain capsule willingly and then drained the glass of water. "Why couldn't it have been my left?"

"Because your left arm wasn't under you, I guess," Melanie said. She sat on the edge of the sofa near his feet.

"Brilliant." Kevin shut his eyes. He could see the sunlight, the ball sailing toward him. He could feel the connection his arm had with the racket like an extension of his body, its natural attack on the moving sphere, the force of his body following, following, just like Bliss had taught him when he was eight. "The summer's ruined," he said, biting the air. "Dammit, I want to play!"

They were hovering around him, Bliss at his head, Melanie at his feet, Wren leaning over the back of the sofa. He waited for them to attempt a miracle, a feeble gesture he could deride and toss back at them with his anger. But they were silent.

"I think you should try to sleep," Bliss said finally.

"Melanie and I have a date," Kevin said, grasping any point of insurrection he could find.

"I can't make it," Melanie said softly. "I'll stay here, though, if you'd like. After you sleep a while, we could watch television, if that's all right with you, Mrs. Jackson."

"It's fine. You stay and have dinner with us."

"Kevin?"

But he was falling, a soft effortless fall so unlike the spill he'd taken earlier. There was nothing to jar him now, no acute spasm of pain cutting his flesh, just the gentle pressure of Melanie's hand through the blanket on his leg, the soft voice of his grandmother and the cool quiet of a familiar place. After a while he'd have to deal with a useless summer, days spent on the sidelines, his mother's divorce, the terrible thing he'd done to his dad and his eventual homecoming. But now he would fall deeper and deeper toward sleep, pillowed with pain medicine. His last thought was that this drifting must be a lot like dying.

Mr. Kensley was in the church study after choir practice Wednesday night. Wren and Jolene saw him behind his desk as they passed on their way home, and Jolene pulled

Wren into the shadows beside the open door and whispered, "Let's go in and talk to him."

"He's busy, Jolene," Wren said.

"I bet he's not," Jolene said. "Besides, we're members of his congregation, aren't we? We ought to be able to go in there and have a conversation."

"About what?"

"I don't know. I'll think of something." Jolene tugged at Wren's arm. "I know, about Kevin. About his breaking his arm and how the doctor says he can't play tennis all summer."

"Jolene, that's dumb."

"You want to see me, girls?" Mr. Kensley called. He was bending over his desk collecting unprinted bulletin papers into one neat stack. "Come on in. Marianne's at a meeting tonight and I'm at loose ends. I'd welcome some company."

Jolene nudged Wren toward the door where they could see Mr. Kensley as blond and golden as a beach boy in his jeans and knit shirt.

"Here, sit," he said, going to draw two folding chairs in front of the desk. "I know this isn't the proper way to chat, across a barricade like this, but it's the best we can do in these cramped quarters. It's a poor communication situation, the kind I was taught to avoid in seminary unless, of course, I want to get the upper hand. Do you think I'll need it?"

"What?" Jolene was flustered, and she crossed her legs so that she could kick one foot to squelch her nerves.

"The upper hand." Mr. Kensley laughed a low chuckle, the kind of laugh that often accompanied sarcasm, the stinging wit Wren had heard among adults that never seemed funny. Still, Mr. Kensley seemed harmless enough, cheerful and hardly older than Kevin.

"Kevin broke his arm," Wren said, seeing that Jolene, for all her hallway bravado, had fallen into a trance. "My brother, Kevin."

"Yes. I know who you mean. I'm sorry I haven't gotten around to visiting every family in the congregation yet. It takes time, you know." Mr. Kensley was looking at her intently. "So," he said, "Kevin has broken his arm. Then I'll put him at the top of my visitation list."

"I wouldn't do that," Jolene blurted out, then turned pink under Mr. Kensley's inquiring eyes. "I mean, Kevin's not very sociable lately. I mean, he's upset over his arm. He's a great tennis player, you know, and the doctor says he's out for the summer. Even after he gets his cast off in about a month, he'll have to do strengthening exercises for a long time before he can really play. It's the saddest thing. I mean, I don't blame him for being depressed and mad with everybody." Jolene stopped short, having exhausted breath and information at the same moment.

"So he's not taking it very well," Mr. Kensley said, looking back at Wren. "It's a big disappointment to him, and there are times when disappointments are harder to take than at other times, if you know what I mean."

So Grandmother has been here, Wren thought, and for a moment, understanding moved visibly between her and the minister. His eyes told her he knew about her parents, had been privy to the family secret even Jolene didn't know.

"Wren, your grandmother is a delightful woman," Mr. Kensley said to confirm her suspicion.

"You should see her mother," Jolene said, desperate to

participate. She could sense the conversation edging away from her. "She's a knockout."

"Maybe sometime I will," Mr. Kensley said. "And I'll drop in on Kevin. Maybe you girls will be there, too. We don't want a visit from the minister to put him off."

"Thanks." Wren got up to leave. She felt tired, as though she'd been talking for hours.

Jolene got up, too, but reluctantly as if she hadn't had her chance yet.

"Good night, girls. Thanks for stopping by." Mr. Kensley was directing them into the dark hallway. "Can you see your way out?"

"We know the way," Wren said. "Good night."

Under the porch light on the side stoop of the building, Jolene pulled Wren to her. "Why didn't you keep talking? We never did find out anything about him!"

"I thought it was Kevin you were concerned about." Wren went down the steps.

"What's that song you sing sometimes? When I'm not with the one I love, I love the one I'm with?" Jolene sighed. "I guess that means I'm fickle."

"Or maybe you don't love anybody yet."

"But I wish I did! I swear, Wren, I want to so bad!"

"Well, it's not all fun," Wren said. She stopped under the street light from which she and Jolene would take different directions.

"You mean you don't like having Sam Holland at your beck and call?"

"I don't know exactly what I mean," Wren said. "But just look at Mother and Daddy. They must have been so beautiful together once. Everybody thought they were perfect, and look what happened. And now here's Kevin with Melanie trying so hard and Kevin so wrapped up in his own problems, he hardly sees her. Maybe things just don't work out the way we hope they will, no matter how hard we try."

"I don't believe that about you and Sam," Jolene said, grasping at the last thread of romance floating by. "I bet you'll be just the ones to live happily ever after."

Wren went home, hearing Jolene's words in her head. They were foolish, she knew, but somehow their hopefulness filled her with expectations. She felt suddenly buoyant, unhampered for a moment by Kevin's despair.

When she reached home, she knew she could put her fingers over the familiar squares of the telephone digits and press the sequence that brought Sam to her. She would hear his voice instantly, before the completion of the first ring, as if he had been waiting with his hand on the receiver.

"How are you?" he would say. And she would be all right.

Chapter 12

 Wren practiced the piano for two hours early every morning in the summer, the hours when Kevin had always been on the tennis court. After tennis he'd always come home to shower and change before going to the drugstore where he worked until mid-afternoon. Now, with his arm in a cast, he slept late, went to work groggy and irritable, and stayed until late when his grandfather closed up.

Wren was learning Chopin's *Fantasie Impromptu,* and the light floating notes drifted up the stairs and into Kevin's head while he slept so that when she made a mistake, he sometimes awoke abruptly to the discord, then grimaced into his pillow and covered his head against the repetition of the fragment. He wished she wouldn't practice while he was at home, but he had never said that to her. Why should her day be disrupted just because his summer was ruined?

Besides, occasionally he liked to wake up to the music, especially the cantabile movement which he knew had the same melody as an old popular tune he'd heard his grandmother sing. But more often than not, the music irritated him with the fact that Wren still had too good arms, two useful hands, ten fingers that worked, while he carried around this cast, dirty and smeared with inky autographs. He'd considered sponging it with water to get the letters off, make it pristine and unmarred by witty condolences, but he knew water would ruin the plaster.

He didn't want to go through getting a new cast because he didn't want to see his arm yet. He dreamed about it, though. Saw it vividly in a nightmare of twisted bruised flesh, a white branch of bone sticking through, his wrist permanently angled into uselessness. Once he'd awakened crying over the sight of it, and Bliss had put her arms around him, snuggling his head to her breasts like his mother used to. He had thought for a moment that the arms were his mother's, and he'd leaned into her, soaking up comfort.

When he was younger, eleven or twelve, he had thought about being in an accident—something temporarily deforming. Once he'd almost turned his bike into the side of a slow-moving car. He had wanted to. But his inability to accurately evaluate the outcome had, at the last moment, caused him to respond to the blare of the frantic horn and he'd swung the other way, into the curb where he caught his balance with one bare foot on the concrete edge and watched the car moving away, down the street with its elderly, nerve-wracked passengers.

Self-preservation had saved him. He knew from reading the papers that freakish moments of unsuspecting happenstance could turn into disasters: children drowned in bathtubs; a bumped head could cause cerebral hemorrhage; a thorn prick might turn into blood poisoning. So, preoccupied with risk as he mentally courted accidents, he had been forced to see the dreadful possibilities of gangrene, wheelchairs, severed bone. His covert mental glances at injury eventually worried him into fright so that, at twelve, he was temporarily afraid to ride his bike. He would lean against the back seat of Bliss' car pressing an imaginary brake pedal and anxiously perusing the unpredictable traffic. He backed off from baseballs that curved across the plate, abandoned his bow-and-arrow set, put his Boy Scout knife in a drawer. But even in his fear, he had believed that a crushed leg or collarbone would make Karen come back. Now, at sixteen, he knew a broken wrist hadn't.

Melanie was in the drugstore almost every day, pushing her cousin's infant in a collapsible stroller and pulling the three-year-old sibling along with bribes of fountain sodas and ice cream cones to keep him docile.

She would come midafternoon while the baby was still drowsy and content from her nap and would park the stroller beside the little boy who sucked happily on a straw while she wandered down the aisles to find Kevin. He would be in the hair products or dental hygiene departments, stocking shelves with his left hand.

She came down the aisle and before he ever saw her, she was working on making her voice and face bright. When he looked up, she was always smiling, ready to be cheerful as if she were a medication he took—bottled brightness, a sunny disposition acquired by spoon. But it wearied her. She felt worn down every afternoon as she knelt beside him in the aisle, watching his careful placement of shampoo or hair spray in neat rows, and put her arm around his shoulder. He was tense. She felt him half shrug away while his face turned toward hers, laying a soft, almost touchless kiss on her lips.

"I want to go to the tractor pull Saturday," she said, catching his cheek with her lips, then edging briefly down the side of his mouth. "Wren and Sam are going. The Hollands are obviously into that sort of thing."

"I don't know," Kevin said.

"Please come," Melanie said, standing up while he stayed squatting on the floor beside his carton. "I don't want to go by myself. The volunteer fire department is sponsoring it so part of the admission price goes to a good cause. We'll have a good time, I promise."

He didn't want to go anywhere, hadn't wanted to be around people since his accident, but he knew she deserved something from him, a return on her investment.

"All right, I'll go."

"Thanks, Kevin. I've got to see about the kids. This baby-sitting is for the birds!" She touseled his hair gently. "Call me later."

"I may go straight to bed."

"I'll call you then, and get you up." She hurried down the aisle, tanned legs in white shorts, sandals slapping, arms swinging. She was so perfect while he felt so used up.

"I'll call you," he said almost too softly for her to hear. "Just don't expect too much."

Kneeling there amid the cartons of stock, he wondered if anyone could expect anything worthwhile from him again. That was why he hadn't been able to tell Melanie or his grandparents what happened when he went to see his dad. They would never forgive him, especially not Bliss, although she knew all about positive reinforcement and would pretend to understand that his telling his father had been inadvertent. But she wouldn't forgive because the injured party was her son whom she would always protect, even against his own child.

So he had told Wren just this morning. Told her and left her with it, a grenade of guilt and remorse clutched in her hand to prevent its exploding in his own. He shouldn't have told her, and yet there had been some comfort in her quiet response.

"Oh, Kevin," she had said as if her concern were for all of them. She felt grief for their condition more than for what it had caused him to do. "If he'd had a serious setback, the doctor would have called us, so he must be well enough to handle it. Somebody had to tell him, Kevin."

But not me, Kevin thought, turning back to the hair spray. It shouldn't have been me.

When the three of them arrived at the fairgrounds, Wren saw that the Hollands were already there. She motioned to Kevin and Melanie to follow her, and they went across the field of newly mowed grass where Sam was leaning against his father's pickup, drinking a Dr Pepper. They were surrounded by trucks, all driven close to the track for a good view.

"Where's Paul and the tractor?" Wren asked him.

"Down at the end of the track somewhere," Sam said. "Paul means business at this thing. The prize money for his class is three hundred dollars."

"What class is he in?" Kevin wanted to know. He and Melanie leaned against the truck, Kevin with his good arm around her while they looked at the assortment of tractors gathered near the starting line.

"The 110 to 130 horsepower. Dad got a new John Deere

last year and that's what he's running. We didn't even bring the little tractor, so it's all or nothing on Beulah."

"Beulah?" Wren stepped up on the fender to see over the other trucks.

"Yeah." Sam laughed, wrapping his arm around her knees to keep her steady. "Dad used to farm with mules, and they all had names. So when he started buying tractors, he thought he ought to name them, too. Makes it a little more personal. You get to know a tractor if you sit on it all day while it works for you, just like you get to know a mule if you walk behind one far enough. We've got Beulah and Maud. Used to have Dixie, named after Dad's favorite mule when he was a boy, but she died."

"The mule?" Melanie asked.

"I'm sure the mule did, but I was referring to the tractor." Sam lifted Wren down. "You want to stand on the bed? Beats your fancy balancing act up there."

"If that's all right."

"That's why Mom pulled it up here. She'll be back in a minute. She's off visiting."

Jolene joined them on the truck bed, pulling herself up and slapping the dust off her jeans. "I swear, this is the dirtiest place!"

"Not yet, it's not. You wait until those tractors start slinging dust. Then you'll think dirt," Sam said. "Of course, this is a little pull if you compare it to the ones we go to in the fall. Right now, all the farmers have their tractors in the field, and they don't want to bring them in, even on Saturday. We wouldn't be in this one except that Paul wanted to run it. He's not home in the fall, anyway.

But that's when the souped-up tractors enter and stakes get even higher."

"Looks like they're getting ready to start," Kevin said.

They all looked out at the hard dirt straightaway that stretched close to a quarter of a mile in front of them. A blue Ford tractor had pulled up to the beginning of the track, and men were attaching a metal sled to it. The sled was flat on the front so that it rested on the ground, but the rear end had four wheels. A metal weight lay on the sled above the wheels, resting on two cables attached to the rear axle of the sled.

"As the tractor pulls the sled forward, the weight moves toward the front of the sled. That makes the weight greater and the tractor has to pull harder," Sam said to Jolene, who was staring at the contraption as if it were a new form of torture. "When the weight is all the way to the front of the sled, it triggers an air horn so we know the tractor is pulling the maximum load. If more than one tractor pulls the entire distance, they put more weight on the sled—usually a little tractor—and pull again. Of course, some of them stall before they get that far."

"Well, I just think this is the dumbest thing!" Jolene began and then leaned beyond the truck railing to watch the first tractor gearing up to pull. "Will you just look at that!" she said when the tractor stalled, wheels spinning holes in the dirt and gears grinding. "Why, he's no good at this at all!"

"I thought you said this was dumb," Wren said.

"Well it is, but as long as they're going to do it, they ought to get it right!"

They watched the second tractor attached to the load move onto the track and pull just past the spot where the Ford spun out.

"So far he's got it," Kevin said. Dust blew high into their faces.

"I'm going to start sneezing," Melanie said.

"That's nothing new," Kevin said, looking sour. "I thought you said you were going to be over that in June."

"I am over it," Melanie said, "unless I get in a dust bowl."

"Go get in the cab then," Kevin said, regretting his sharpness. He wished he didn't feel angry all the time. He touched her arm. "I'll come, too."

Wren was peering through the dust at the track. "Look at the holes they're making, Sam. Won't they affect Paul's chances?"

"The first tractors have an advantage. Paul will have to stay out of the ruts, but sometimes there's no way to avoid them."

"Look at that one!" Jolene squealed, eyeing the Holland's new tractor. "And look at that hunk driving it! I vote for him already! Come on, John Deere!"

Sam and Wren laughed. "What do you think?" she asked.

"He's got a good chance."

"Look!" Jolene was slapping the top of the cab. "He's going for it! He's doing it!"

They listened to the engine roar, heard the grinding gears, saw the weight slipping forward through the churning dust as the tractor pulled down the track.

"Steady, stea-dy," Sam said under his breath. "Hold on and you've got it."

The horn pierced the dust with its squawk and still the tractor heaved forward.

"He won!" Jolene yelled, bouncing on the truck bed and shaking her fists in the air. "I'm going down there right now!" She jumped off the tailgate and raced through the flying dust to where Paul had stopped the tractor.

"I thought she didn't like dust and noise," Sam said.

"She doesn't, but she'd go through a sandstorm to get to a man."

The last tractor in Paul's class was cranking up.

"Here comes Mom," Sam said and went to give her a hand up onto the truck bed.

"Hello, Wren," Kathryn said. "He ran fine, didn't he, Sam?"

"I don't think that Wallace's Allis-Chalmers can beat him," Sam said. "I've seen it pull before."

Melanie and Kevin got out of the cab. "We're going to get a drink," Kevin said. "You folks want something?"

"We'll wait," Wren said.

"Well, we're not staying much longer. Maybe through one more class. The dust makes Melanie's allergies act up just when I thought they were dying a natural death. You two want to come back to town with us?"

"If Dad can pick me up at Wren's house later," Sam said, looking at Kathryn. "What do you think, Mom?"

"I think the truck ought to know the way to the Jackson house without a driver," Kathryn said as she put her arm around Wren. "You're sure you want to put up with this boy? I know what a nuisance he can be."

"Oh, Mom."

"You should see him wandering around the house at night, waiting for the phone to ring. Either that or he's plastered to it. Any day now there's going to be a receiver growing out of his ear. His dad says working all day must not sap enough of his energy; we need to find him a night job just to keep him off his feet. He's just pacing and fidgeting. I say to him, 'Watch a little TV. Read a book. Look at the stars, for heaven's sake.' But he's not interested. Just got one interest now."

"Mother," Sam groaned.

"And now I've gone and embarrassed him. That's what happens when you get my age and start saying the truth. People look at you funny, think you're batty in the head. Your children don't bring their friends around near often enough. They're worried you're going to sit between them on the sofa or get the baby pictures out."

Wren giggled while Sam looked pained.

"I'm shutting up," Kathryn said, giving Wren a hug, "but you get him to bring you out to the farm again. You're welcome anytime."

They turned to watch the last tractor pulling the weight. Just before the load reached the air horn, the tractor began to lose traction.

"I think Paul's won," Kathryn said.

"Look who's coming." Wren laughed.

Paul sprinted through the dust with Jolene running behind him. He took off his cowboy hat and wiped grime off his forehead with his handkerchief. A cloud of dust settled on him and drifted back on Jolene. "I guess I got it, Mom." He grinned.

Jolene parked herself beside him. "You didn't tell me he's your brother," she called up to Sam. "I swear I'm the last to know everything around here!"

"Jolene," Wren said, motioning for her to stretch up so they could whisper. "He's too old for you. He's in college."

"I know. Somewhere between Kevin and Mr. Kensley. Isn't it perfect?"

"Jolene, he's nineteen," Wren said.

"And I'm fourteen since November. I'm absolutely months older than you, Wren. Why, if Mama'd cheated a little, I could be a year ahead of you in school and you know it, so I'll just catch whoever I can." Jolene sidled up to Paul, who leaned away from her and the truck to spit out a quick, straight stream of tobacco juice.

"Aren't you just dying for a soft drink?" she asked. "I know you are."

"A beer," Paul said to the rest of them. He wasn't exactly ignoring Jolene, but he wasn't singling her out either.

"And a hot dog," Jolene suggested, finagling a spot between him and the rest of the world. "I'll go with you to get it."

"We're going back to town soon," Sam said. "Don't you want to come with us, Jolene?"

"Oh no, I think I'll hang around here for a while," Jolene said, rolling her eyes in Paul's direction. "I'll get a ride somehow. I just think this tractor pull is the most exciting thing I've ever seen!"

They watched her following Paul into the crowd on his

way to the concession stand. Because the sun was low, its pink glow struck them full in the face, and they squinted into the pearly dust to see Jolene latch on to Paul's belt loop and pull herself up beside him.

"How long do you think he'll put up with her?" Wren asked Sam and his mother.

"Until he meets up with Janice Barker, I reckon," Kathryn said. "They've got a date at nine o'clock, when she gets off from the A & P."

"Poor Jolene," Wren said.

"Poor Jolene nothing. Paul's the one I'm worrying about," Sam said.

"Well, I'm not worrying about a thing." Kathryn sighed. "Paul's got three hundred dollars he didn't have this morning and the tractor's in one piece. Now you children go enjoy your Saturday night. They don't come but once a week, you know."

Wren and Sam found Kevin and Melanie and got a ride back to town.

"We could go to the movies or something," Melanie said, as if she were in charge of the evening's entertainment. "Or play miniature golf."

"Yeah," Kevin said, "where I'll get a hole in one with my left hand."

"Sorry, Kevin. Well, we could go cruising or play cards—"

"I'm taking them home," Kevin said. "Unless"—he leaned back and turned partially toward Wren and Sam— "you want me to put you out downtown."

"We'll go home," Wren said, glancing at Sam, who didn't seem concerned about either alternative.

They went up the front walk, and Wren got out her key.
"Grandmother and Granddaddy are out, but they'll be back
in a couple of hours." She turned the key and the lock
released, freeing the door. "Come in."

The house was shadowed, and she switched on a lamp in
the hall and then one in the living room. "We could watch
television or get something to eat. Or both," she said.

"In a minute." Sam pulled her into his arms.

The mantel clock ticked. It seemed to Wren they had
automatically become part of the quiet. Their presence
wasn't disruptive to the house but seemed to fill up a space
naturally, as though this were where they belonged. She
didn't feel awkward or nervous being alone with him.

He kissed the corner of her mouth, then along her jaw,
past her ear to her temple, light dry kisses that made her
hold back a shiver.

"I love you," she heard him whisper. His lips traced her
forehead, fell gently on her closed eyes, then to her mouth.
She parted her lips under his. She felt so comfortable, so
trusting of him, just the way Bliss had once told her loving
someone could be.

"You won't be embarrassed or shy when it's the right
person," Bliss had said to help her through the awkwardness
of first dances and Christmas parties in basement family
rooms. "You'll know when someone cares about you in a
special way and when you feel the same."

Listening to her grandmother, she had envisioned an
imaginary person, someone as sweet as Robbie Benson, as
handsome as Warren Beatty, as unattainable as Robert
Redford—but here was Sam instead, his touch wonderfully
delicate on her bare arms, his cool fingertips like water

spilling slowly on her neck. She could smell him, the dusty fairground scent infusing on his damp chest with a hint of British Sterling. She thought no one had ever been so real to her or so close, although she sensed a familiarity in her happiness, as if she could remember a similar sensation from long ago, perhaps from her mother's arms or her father's hand on her back as he balanced her on a bike. They had kept her safe once, just like Sam would now. He would never want anything but the best for her.

She lifted her arms around him, pulling him toward her, trusting all her knowledge of him, but he retreated slightly and breathed against her cheek and into her hair.

"Play the piano for me, will you?" he whispered.

"Right now?"

"I think you'd better." He let her go.

Then he faced her, leaning against the side of the piano while she played the first movement of *Moonlight Sonata*. She played from memory so that she could watch him intermittently. His presence pulled her away from the music, bore into her concentration. She knew she wasn't playing well, but she didn't care. Tomorrow at practice, without distractions, no smile easing into the edges of her mouth, she would play it properly, just to prove to herself she could.

At practice she would envision a familiar scene, herself on a stage wearing a severe black gown, alone with an ebony piano, the audience separated from her by the footlights. She was day and the audience night, until the music—her playing—joined them in a dawning light above the pit. The music would connect them, and yet there would always be that necessary distance. She would never see their faces or let them interfere like Sam was doing.

Chapter Twelve

She stopped and released the pedal. The room was abruptly quiet.

"I can't believe how well you play," Sam said, not knowing how his face tempted her toward mediocrity.

She rippled an arpeggio up the keyboard and then struck a final chord. "I intend to major in piano and organ," she said and waited. The words seemed to embody themselves on the chord, become powerful and concrete between them.

"So you can play the church organ and teach music like your grandmother," Sam said.

What had she expected? Her own vision of herself to cross his eyes? How could he know words she had never spoken to anyone until now?

"No," she said. "In concert. On a stage. That's where I want to play."

"Oh," he said.

She rose from the bench, feeling foolish in her jeans and dusty shirt. How could she expect him to see? And yet, having heard her play, she had thought he would. She turned away, remembering that once only a few weeks ago she'd asked him for a vision of their future and had accepted what he saw. She had wanted it because it sounded so lovely, so safe.

"So," he said, putting his hands on her shoulders.

She willed herself to hold straight and still so that he would feel the tension in her arms, the disappointment in her shoulders, but instead his fingers running lightly down her arms set off an internal crumbling. Walls sagged and fell outward in shivers, leaving her clean inside, empty of doubt.

She turned to him, saw the piano behind him shimmering in the lamplight and closed her eyes to kiss him. She moved closer to him, pressing her mouth to his, letting herself, at least for this moment, be just any girl learning about love.

Chapter 13

There was something different about her father this time. Wren saw it as he stepped out of the car, one foot extended to the pavement, a hand gripping the rim of the open window. He came into the light, his face looking pale and subdued beside his mother's rich tan, small beside her. Suddenly he looked up and saw Wren and was striding away from Bliss with an energetic gait as if he were about to take off running.

He bounded up the steps to where Wren waited on the stoop, front door left ajar to ease him in. He opened his arms to her, clamping her to his debilitated body, but she could feel him taking on power right there as his arms tightened around her. She transfused him, his bony hollow chest rising hard against her cheek.

"You are the prettiest sight!" he said. "Seems like years since I've seen you!" He meant since he'd seen her at home. The past months in the hospital were now abnegated, an unmentionable loss.

"How are you, Daddy?"

"I'm good, Wren. Really good." He released her, and they turned to see Bliss getting his bag out of the car. "I think I've got a grip on a lot of things this time, honey. Now I've just got to get through this adjustment stage. I know there have to be some rough moments, but I intend to improve my appetite, play a little tennis, start seeing people. Get back to work. Thank God I've got that office space above the drugstore. Any landlord but my own dear dad would have kicked me out long ago."

"I'll get that, Grandmother," Wren said and left his arms to pick up the suitcase. Maybe alone in the yard, at a distance from his volatile intensity, she could be objective. Her head reeled with the possibility that he was truly cured, impervious to moods, symptomatic headaches, and nausea. Maybe then her mother would come back, or they would all go to Chicago together. A small germ of hopefulness wormed in her head, threatening her because she couldn't afford to believe him. Already she felt smothered by his euphoria. She sensed how his excitement intruded on reality.

And yet he had never come home so confident before. Other times had found him restless and apologetic for having been a burden. Either that or slightly belligerent, as if he couldn't cope with the fact of his own absence. Either Kevin had grown taller, Bliss had changed the color of a chair or served an unfamiliar dish, or Wren had won a piano competition he couldn't remember being told about. Those were the moods she was used to, and now here was another one, this jubilance she didn't know how to respond to.

Wren followed them into the house and took the bag up to his room. She could hear him talking to Grandmother downstairs, a constant nervous stream of words assaulting their well-kept silence. The voices slowly moved away, down the hall toward the kitchen. His room was quiet now. Bliss had brought flowers in from the garden and books from the shelves downstairs, recent issues of the *National Geographic,* a new biography of Gary Cooper. She had put out his Bible, too, a worn, tattered King James version that he'd used through his adolescence.

Wren sat down on the bed and opened the book, her fingers slipping over the thin curling pages, seeing asterisks in the margins, passages blocked in red ink, verses underlined. She could imagine him as a boy doing Bible drill in Vacation Bible School, thumbs touching the red edge of the Psalms as he waited anxiously for book, chapter, and verse to be called. She traced her finger down a thumb-printed page, then turned to the Gospels where the pages were even more abused. Part of Matthew was loose, worn through at the binding, and she slipped the pages back into the fold.

Had he depended so much on this Bible? she wondered. Were these obligatory assignments, or had he turned the pages on his own, searching with troubled, guilty dedication, his mind still open to the possibility of words? She passed over Revelations and the book lay open at the torn backsheet. There, written in a tiny awkward hand, obscure and forgotten, she read *Tom loves Jesus* and under it, even smaller, *And Lorinda Peterson.*

Wren smiled and closed the book gently, as if to protect the words against further damage. Now she saw him at training union in line behind a girl name Lorinda, inconspicuously fingering a soft curl that fell down her back; saw them sharing a hymnal, fingers touching on the binding; saw his shoulder against hers as they sat on the back pew, writing notes on the margins of bulletins, their eyes scanning the pews near them for suspicious, disapproving glances. She saw Kevin.

"Is he here?" he asked from the doorway. "Where is he?"

"In the kitchen with Grandmother." Wren put the Bible on top of the other books and stood up.

"Well, what do you think?" Kevin asked, coming in.

"I don't know. He's different."

"Of course he's different. He's not a zombie. They don't let zombies come home."

"I mean he's different from any first day I can remember. He was talking about going back to work and playing tennis. I think he's really well, Kevin."

"It's a new drug," Kevin said. "It's always a new drug."

"Well, maybe this one works. We have to hope it will."

"I don't have to. By the time Mom gets here next week, he'll be in the dumps. You can count on it."

"Not if we help him, Kevin."

"I don't want to help him. I'm tired of helping him. When's he going to help me? Sometimes I wish they'd just keep him."

"You don't mean that, Kevin. You can't mean that."

"Her, too. I wish neither of them would ever come here again. I wish they'd just leave us alone."

"Kevin!"

"A welcoming committee right in my room," Tom said. He came toward them, shoulders sagging a little. He worked his hands nervously in his pockets. The afternoon seemed to be wearing him down already. Even now, his old life impinged on his new beginning. He glanced around the room before looking straight at Kevin. "Well, son. Here we are again."

"Yes, sir."

"Sorry about your arm. Your grandmother says another month in the cast?"

"Yes, sir."

"Well, a month isn't very long. Unless you're in a cast." Tom smiled at Wren, looking for support.

"The doctor said maybe he can play a little in August," she said.

"Maybe." Kevin rubbed his hand across the cast as if they were threatening it. Their hopefulness seemed like a menace to him.

"Still seeing that Washburn girl?" Tom was searching his memory for something to say to his son. What could they talk about that didn't remind them both of lost time, broken bonds?

"Melanie," Kevin said. "Yes, sir."

"And you, Wren? I hear you have a boyfriend. A summer romance, is it? Who did your grandmother say—John Holland's boy?"

"Sam."

"Named for his grandfather, I expect. I remember old Mr. Sam. Did you know I used to go out there when John and I were boys? Mr. Sam took us on a hayride once on the back of an old pickup he had. Told us when we were getting on that he had one requirement—all the girls had to get on one side of the truck and all the boys on the other. You should have heard the ruckus in that hay when we got down the road a little ways and it was dark. I thought I'd never find my girl. When everybody finally got settled down, we could hear him up in the cab just laughing at us. I remember we started singing. There was a high moon, a white summer moon, and we were singing and scratching in that itchy bed of hay. Between singing to make Mr. Sam think we were behaving, and scratching, we hardly had time for anything else."

"That's a terrific story, Daddy," Wren said, going to hug him.

His embrace was different in this room, more tender and clinging than the powerful bear hug he'd given her downstairs. He looked over her head at Kevin.

"I wish I had a story about the Washburns," he said. "I suppose I could make up something."

"Shouldn't you rest, Dad?" Kevin asked.

"I'd rather be with you two," Tom said, "unless you want to get away. I wouldn't blame you."

Wren looked at Kevin, willing him to want to stay.

"I've got a little time," he said.

"And a hug?" Tom asked. "Got a hug for your old man?"

Wren watched her brother come toward them, the tentative steps, his embarrassed body pulling itself in to avoid more than peripheral contact.

It's all right, she said silently to him. We're here together now. She held out her hand to catch him. Her fingers pulled him in, feeling as they did the backward strain of muscle, tight tendons, his warm flushed skin.

Come, Kevin, she said to him through soundless lips. She gripped his waist, leaving his good arm free for their father. The men, equal in height and size, caught each other, then drew Wren in with them, her shoulders crushed between them in their apprehensive embrace.

Bliss watched her son sleeping. She stood in the open doorway, startled by the sight of him there, his long thin legs sticking out of white boxer shorts, his back bony and frail, like a child whose height had suddenly spurted beyond his normal weight. She remembered suddenly how he had looked at thirteen and fourteen, recalled those same meatless arms and legs. He had lifted weights, chinned door frames, drained milkshakes at the drugstore, forked down potatoes, demanded steaks. Still he had been slow filling out, had aggravated her with endless advertisements on back covers of comic books, worried that his nose was too big.

It *had* been much too big for one winter when he was especially gaunt and neglected-looking. A Pinocchio nose, he'd said seriously, and she had been struck by the sudden facial similarity he had with her cousin Jess, whose face had never grown to compatible size with his nose.

An elephant trunk, a pig's snout, Tom had joked to prevent their jokes. She had been so worried about him, had actually prayed that her beautiful child be mercifully spared Jesse's Durante-like schnoz. By summer, when Tom was tanned and healthy, ten pounds of steak and potatoes padding his angular frame, his nose seemed to find a regular proportion. His face was familiar again, and she breathed easier.

Now, watching him sleep, she found herself barely breathing at all, air sucked in and exploding in her chest.

She saw how he was that boy again. She recognized the spindly form and felt memories of his childhood like an ache. She wanted to pray again, like she had when his nose panicked her with its gargantuan proportions. She needed some simple one-sentence intercession that would comfort her and tell her she was doing all she could.

One must love one's children when they are ugly, dumb, obnoxious, even villainous. One did love them, against all odds and most intensely in moments of strife when the child couldn't possibly believe there was love anywhere. When Tom doubted himself, he always seemed to doubt her first. He had been testing her for years. Will you love me if I close the office at noon? Will you care if I don't get up this morning? Will you feed me, wash me, hide me from public view, even from my own children's terrified eyes?

That was what he expected of her.

"What is it, Grandmother?" Kevin whispered behind her.

"Sh-h-h." She backed into the hall and drew the door closed. "I just woke up and wanted to check on him. He seemed so well in the afternoon, but I thought he was a little restless at dinner."

"He's fine," Kevin said. "You ought to go back to bed. It's three o'clock."

"What are you doing up?" Bliss whispered, taking his arm as they went quietly down the hall. She paused outside his room.

"I heard you, I guess. I woke up knowing something was going on in the house. Maybe it's just Dad's being home. Another spirit at large or something like that."

"And next week your mother will be here, too." Bliss

sighed, rubbing her hands on her chilled arms. "I don't know if any of us are ready."

"What difference will that make? She'll come anyway," Kevin said, slipping into his room. He shut the door soundlessly.

Bliss went down the hall where Bill was sleeping and lay down beside him. The house settled again. She listened. They were all here, safely under her roof. In rooms lining the hall like a garrison, her children slept, dreamed, conquered their demons in the dawning light. She lay there a long time, her mind moving to and fro, catching a vision of Wren at two, Kevin at six; backward to her infant Tom, then as a boy of eight hauling in a brook trout; his wedding day; the morning he first held Kevin in his arms.

Toward dawn, she got up again, pulled on her robe, and went to Kevin's door. There seemed to be an urgency in her need to see him, her broken-boned child, her ravaged sleeping angel who in the daylight would once again be sullen with anger and impossible to reach. She stood in the shadowy bluish light, holding her arms across her chest, hand at the pulse in her throat, and saw that he looked like Tom.

Chapter 14

Wren and Jolene tried on shorts in Broad-hurst's Department Store.

"I just know I'm not going to find a thing in here," Jolene said, turning from the mirror to get a glimpse of her backside. "There's not a single thing in this place that fits me right."

"Those look fine to me," Wren said, picking through the pile of clothes the clerk had let them bring into the dressing room.

"They do not! They're too big in the legs. Look here!" Jolene held out the sides of the pants, like a little girl showing off her Sunday dress. She unzipped the shorts and slipped out of them. "Let's go to that boutique down the street. They've got the cutest things in there."

"I don't have time." Wren held a pair of drawstring shorts up to her waist and studied them in the mirror. "I'm meeting Sam in thirty minutes." She glanced at her watch. "Twenty minutes now."

"And you're abandoning me. You said you'd help me pick out shorts and tops and now you're quitting before I find a thing that looks right!" Jolene shimmied into white shorts that sported a navy-and-red belt. "What about these?"

"They fit, Jolene."

"I look like the flag." Jolene pouted. "I should get a blouse with stars on it and be a Fourth of July decoration. Let's go one more place, Wren, just one more."

"We've been three places already, Jolene, and you've put on at least ten pairs of shorts that looked perfect."

"Nothing looks perfect on me," Jolene said, riffling through the shorts she'd discarded on the floor, "but I kinda like these." They were exactly like the ones Wren was trying on. "But you're getting them! I know you are."

"We can both get them, Jolene. I'll get these yellow ones and you can take the blue ones."

"I don't want the same as you," Jolene said irritably.

"Last summer you didn't mind if we dressed alike. Last summer we had three identical outfits except for color, and it was your idea."

"Last summer," Jolene said, wiggling into her own jeans and jerking up the zipper, "last summer we went everywhere together. Last summer we were just like sisters, only better because we weren't really sisters. But it's not the same anymore." Jolene looked at Wren through the mirror.

"You mean because of Sam," Wren said. She saw them both full-length, the white edges of flesh around the cups of Jolene's bra, her own lean, tanned body growing supple in places, exaggerated it seemed to her by the mirror's slight distortion. They looked so much the same, curly brown hair, the same array of chains glinting on their chests, the same shade of polish on their toenails, the same color in their cheeks.

But they were different. She knew that and yet she didn't want to agree, couldn't force out words that would separate them even more from everything shared, all the hours they'd spent going places and doing things. Even more than that, the hours they'd spent doing nothing—but always knowing they could depend on each other to be there. There was so much past between them, so many foolish secrets, such intimacy, so much frantic attention paid each other as if only the two of them mattered in the world.

But now Sam mattered. He counted in hours, in words, in touches. He could know things Jolene did not.

"You will always be my best friend," Wren said to her. She grinned. "Next year I bet you'll have half the boys in high school after you. We'll double-date and then sleep over just like always. I promise, Jo."

"Don't make promises you can't keep," Jolene said, averting her face. She slipped into her shirt and tucked the tail in her jeans. "Well, I'm getting these," she said, "and these." She swung the shorts under her arm and took her purse off the wall hook. "See you later."

Wren stepped out of the yellow shorts and stood in her underwear in front of the mirror. She remembered the first time she and Jolene had come shopping together without adult interference. It was in this same dressing room or else the one next door where they'd giggled over see-through blouses and seductively brief bikinis they would have never worn in front of anyone but each other. They had bought their eighth-grade prom dresses together just two months ago, the clerk hovering about them with her list of requirements phoned in from home. They had to be on-the-shoulder styles with fitted waists, none of that clingy jersey stuff with their breasts shoved out of an Empire bodice. The dresses they ended up with were old-fashioned and a little girlish, but they didn't mind since they would look the same.

"Did you find something, dear?" the clerk asked, holding back the curtain to peep in at Wren who, drawing her shirt in front of her body, turned away both from the clerk and the mirror.

"Yes. I'm coming," she said, her voice muffled as the cotton passed over her head.

The clerk disappeared, and the curtain again secluded Wren in the tiny, littered vault. She stepped into her jeans and pulled them up over her hips, then sat down on the stool to slip on her shoes. Her fingers made quick, tight knots and then she sat there amid the clutter of discarded clothes and stared at the pin-marred partition in front of her.

She heard the jangle of hangers hitting each other from the next cubicle, an exasperated sigh of disapproval; she saw a shirt drop to the floor, then heard the metal clips sliding on the rod as the curtain flew open and the woman left, leaving the shirt where it lay. She was alone, enveloped in discards. Abandoned. She was almost fourteen, only a few weeks from her birthday. In less than three months she would be going to high school, changing classes, joining clubs, finding her niche. She knew all that would happen as naturally as the changing weather, as easily as turning the pages of her calendar. Probably this fourteenth year of her life would mean growing away from Jolene in ways almost unnoticeable to her. Toward Sam. She could feel herself drawn to him just as the hand on her watch moved closer to three when he would be waiting at the drugstore. This year, she would begin to take on another existence, perhaps make decisions that would affect the rest of her life. The prospect frightened her a little, and yet she marveled at it, too. There was no reason to fear this beginning, and so she stood up, stared at herself for a long critical moment in the mirror and then turned away, heading for Sam.

Father's Day. Tom in his Sunday suit on his way to church with them, walking between his son and daughter, a red rose on his lapel, his hand in Wren's, like she was a child to be led. She did the leading, held him back at the street crossing, urged him forward with her fingers when the light changed. Up the wide steps she brought him, Kevin dropping a step behind into their pale shadow. He also wore a red rose, still damp from Bliss' American Beauty bush. My father lives.

Kevin found Melanie in the vestibule and took her arm, directing her with a nod past the usher at the sanctuary entrance, past their customary back pew down the aisle to where Bliss and Bill sat. They slipped down a little to make room for Kevin and Melanie and then farther still to make a place for Wren and Tom. Tom was on the end, the straight wooden corner of the pew containing him. Wren linked her arm with his for assurance and with her other hand, found the processional in the hymnal. It seemed strange to be in the congregation, looking up instead of out. She watched the youth choir filing into their seats on the first two rows of the loft. They filled in the empty space her absence created so that Jolene sat next to Cecilia Hendricks whom she despised.

"Aren't you supposed to be up there?" Tom whispered.

"I wanted to sit with you," Wren said and squeezed the inside of his arm, going to the bone.

Mr. Kensley in his robe. He looked out over them, his eyes slightly above their faces, and called them to worship. They stood to sing. Sang. Sat once more. He read the text from Genesis, no creation story this, but the strange and dreadful tale of Abraham's near sacrifice of his son, Isaac. The reading chilled them. What a subject for Father's Day! rippled unspoken through the tense congregation. What manner of minister is this?

But he smiled down on them. Did they not recognize in Abraham's terrifying willingness and his child's unyielding trust, the miracle of faith? Were they not all called to take risks, to shatter their own expectations in order to hear God's voice clearly? And if they took that risk, would they not be, as Abraham had been, blessed with God's true and unfailing presence in their lives?

Wren sighed with relief. Mr. Kensley had not failed her with a soppy exhortation to love one's father or some pitifully sentimental lines by an anonymous daughter-poet that would bring unwelcomed tears to her eyes. No, he had preyed on a subject that lay so far beyond her comprehension that its message now seemed momentarily and miraculously clear. She had loved her father, this man whose fingers now clung to hers, and by doing so, she had risked rejection, denial, indifference. Yet here he was sitting beside her, his madness conquered by her faithfulness. She had survived his knife, loving him anyway, no matter what, because he was her father.

Wedged between Melanie and Bliss, Kevin didn't listen.

He had heard the first few words of Scripture and then had closed his eyes and mind to hear only the sound of Mr. Kensley's voice, like a droning insect near his head.

Not that he had anything against Jack Kensley. He liked him, in fact, as much as you could like somebody you had to be careful with. Kensley had come to see him the week he'd broken his arm, dropping in the way ministers are expected to do just to say hello.

But it had turned out differently from other pastoral visits when Kevin always ducked upstairs as quickly as he could. This time Bliss had ushered the minister into the family room and left him there with Kevin, who was stretched out on the sofa pretending to read *Sports Illustrated*. He had been pretending all week. Pretending it didn't matter about his arm, pretending he hadn't done his dad any harm, pretending he didn't care that Karen hadn't come. Looking over at Kensley, who was settling himself comfortably in a chair, Kevin saw him as another challenge to his facade, and so he was silent, mostly because he really didn't have anything to say. Let this jerk do the talking, he had thought, and Kensley did.

"Broke my shoulder once," he said, rubbing the spot. "Years ago in a motorcyle wreck. I had a Harley-Davidson then, my first big bike. My folks had a fit. Mother was screaming all the time about how I was going to get killed and I just about did. That close," he said, measuring the air between thumb and forefinger. "Contusions, unconscious, the works. Nothing permanent, though, unless you want to count forecasting rain." He released his shoulder.

"You've still got a bike," Kevin commented, glad to see Kensley wanted to talk about himself.

"Yeah. Love the things, and Marianne doesn't mind. We go places together. Went up in the mountains last summer, camped out. She's a good sport. Do you ever go camping?"

"I play tennis, or I used to," Kevin said.

"Yeah, well. I guess you'll play again. You'll just have to spend this summer improving your mind."

"A lousy alternative," Kevin said.

"That's what I thought when I broke my shoulder," Kensley said, leaning forward in the chair as if he were about to make an important point. "Nothing to do for two months, so I started reading. Read most of Steinbeck, Hemingway, a little Faulkner, some Conrad. People like that. Started thinking about things. Got interested in religion—not in being religious, but in the ideas that make people want to believe in something bigger than themselves. It turned out to be a good summer."

Kevin hadn't known what to say, although Mr. Kensley hadn't seemed to notice. He hadn't seemed to expect anything at all from Kevin, and at the front door, he put out his left hand and took Kevin's left hand, as if it were natural to shake hands that way.

It was time to stand for the offertory hymn. Melanie poked the page in front of Kevin's face while he fished change from his pants pocket. Fingers felt a quarter, two nickels, several dimes. He rejected the smaller coins and closed his fingers around the quarter. Down the pew his dad was fumbling with his wallet. He saw the arm stretch out, reach past Wren and Melanie, saw with surprise a hand pushing toward his with a five-dollar bill folded between thumb and finger.

It was a gesture from the past, when he used to hold out

his hand to his father at this particular moment and see pocket change fall into it, sometimes even a crumpled bill. Now he drew the bill from the fingers, clutching it in his own.

When they stood to sing, the notes were blurred, but he mouthed them anyway; surrounding him, the air sang with Wren's rich alto, Bliss' soprano, Melanie's light, whispery tone. The offering plate passed him and he released the bill into it, saw it flutter into the mound of bills and white sealed envelopes. The plate moved into Melanie's hand, then Wren's, then his father's. He watched it go past as the moment solidified for him, becoming as definable and as visual as the heavy brass plate. It was a moment in which he felt explicitly his connection to his parent.

Chapter 15

"What do you want from me?" Bliss asked Karen. She turned to the open cabinet opposite her daughter-in-law, hiding her face toward the metal canisters on the shelf.

"Nothing," Karen said quietly. "You've taken care of my children and never maligned me to them."

"That was for them," Bliss said, turning her stony face back to Karen. She looked at the face, such a gloriously beautiful face, and saw wonderful bones that years ago had been hidden by adolescent plumpness and then pregnancy's natural roundness. Lips perfectly formed, brows arched, lids lined. How could she not have seen eighteen years ago that this was an extraordinarily beautiful woman? "And for you," she added, softening her touch. "We shouldn't have to live forever with wrong choices we made when we were just children."

"I was a child, wasn't I?" Karen looked toward the bay window as if she expected to see a reflection of a younger self. Instead, for an instant, she could see the little house they had remodeled. She could remember for a moment what it was like to know exactly what one wanted, this fabric, this particular paint or shrub. There had been reasons for everything then, supportable opinions. Now she went out of her way not to see the house. "I thought being married would be everything," she said.

"For some women, it is."

"For less and less of them, I think," Karen answered, still looking out the window. "Occasionally I go to parties in Atlanta, and more than a few times I've listened to a man tell his life story over a drink. He'll recount all the significant events of his college life, his job, even personal things that you don't expect or want to hear. Then at the end, he'll say, 'Oh, yes, and I have a wonderful wife and three children.' He hadn't really forgotten about them but they were nevertheless in a separate place, away from what he considered interesting about himself. Why can't a woman do that?"

"You can."

"But there's a price on it, isn't there?"

"There's a price on everything, Karen. I shouldn't have to tell you that."

Karen sighed and turned away from the window. "When will Tom be home?"

"Soon. He's having lunch at the store with Bill. I expect he'll be along after that."

"I assume he received the papers. I know he did since I sent them by registered mail."

"Yes. He looked at them for a few minutes right here at the table and then put them in his desk upstairs. So it's done."

"That was all?" Karen asked. "No reaction?"

"Not that I saw. He's getting quiet again, Karen. Some days he barely speaks to anyone, and his appetite isn't what it was. Of course, it could be a temporary setback. Right now I have to believe it is."

Karen came to the counter so that she was close to Bliss, facing her. "There's no one else, Bliss. I want you to know that. Someday perhaps there will be, but not now."

"I don't like to think about you being alone," Bliss said. "When the time comes, you know we'll understand." She had practiced these lines in her head so often lately, preparing herself for their inevitable use. Now she worried they sounded insincere.

"Tell me about the children."

"They're all right. Kevin is—well, breaking his arm put a damper on his summer, but he seems all right. Wren is like any girl in the throes of romance. She's living on phone calls and Saturday nights. It's very exciting to be around, although sometimes she seems a little uneasy with it. I think she's struggling to figure out exactly what's happening to her. Just part of being almost fourteen, I suppose."

"I'm very proud of them. Thank you, Bliss."

"You had them before I did," Bliss said. "You and Tom gave them a good start."

"But not much of a finish," Karen said. "I know that, Bliss. If there's any blame, I know it's mine. I also know they can't feel about me the way they do about you. I can't expect that of them. I just wish I had more time for them."

"So do they."

"Next summer," Karen said, brightening. "By next summer I should be into the job enough to take some time, maybe even a month. I'll take them on a trip, a real vacation. Maybe to Mexico or even to Europe."

"I think they'd rather just have you for a while. It doesn't have to be an expensive vacation. Your time with them is what matters." Bliss came to the table carrying two salad plates with the lunch she had made.

From upstairs they heard the sudden blare of music. Kevin playing Billy Joel. The bass sent heated, resounding messages down the steps to circle their heads.

"That music," Karen said, shaking her head.

"I don't mind it," Bliss replied. "It's his music, after all. He wouldn't listen to it if it didn't speak his language right now. I don't begrudge him that."

"You're a saint."

"Just a grandmother." Bliss smiled. "Let's have lunch before he realizes you're here. Wren will be home soon, too. She slept over with Jolene, and they're probably getting up about now. There seems to be an inordinate amount of important conversation between those girls after midnight. Sometimes when they're here, I wake up and hear that little buzz of sound. It's as constant as a mosquito. I think to myself, what could they be talking about? And then I know. I remember."

"I had a best friend like that," Karen said. "Sometimes we spent hours reconstructing whole conversations, trying to recall every phrase and look. All night long we lived the day again."

They were quiet while "Glass Houses" pounded at them.

"I wish Kevin had a close friend," Bliss said finally. "He used to. But when he went to high school, he seemed to shun the boys he'd been with. Of course, in a way that seemed natural enough. We all grow up, have new interests, find new friends to share them with. But Kevin just hasn't wanted to bother for some reason. That's why his dating

Melanie Washburn has been such a relief to me. She draws him out a little."

"Is he all right?" Karen asked. "Tell me the truth."

"I think he is," Bliss said. But while she said it, her stomach fluttered slightly and she squeezed her fingers into the napkin on her lap. She wasn't sure.

From upstairs, Kevin looked down and saw the Peugeot parked beside his grandmother's Cadillac. The white-hot sun glare off the roof struck his eyes, and he shielded his face from it, squinting, one eye closed. He had known she was here.

He had sensed her in his sleep as if she had come into his room and touched him. He was grateful she hadn't. He didn't want anyone to see him sleeping, although he wasn't sure that Bliss didn't sometimes stealthily turn the knob to his door while he dreamed and look down on him as he'd seen her do with Tom. She wanted to see for herself that he was sleeping just as when he was younger, she'd wanted to hear him blow his nose, just to make sure he really did it. So sleeping turned into a performance, something he did to make Bliss content, an assurance to her that he was okay.

He dropped his new record on the turntable and touched the needle to it. He heard the crash of glass and then the music spilled out at him, bright splintery shards of sound. They cut into his head, little pricks of recognition.

"You may be right I may be crazy. . . ." The music was too loud, but he lay back on the bed anyway, letting the impetuous driving barrage of guitars and the strident voice strike their stinging blows.

This is who I am, he thought, knowing the music could be heard downstairs where Karen was. There was a brief silence, three seconds of calm and then the almost inaudible buzz of the phone. *"When am I gonna take control get a hold of my emotion . . ."* the voice cried out. He felt assaulted, even abused by the fierceness of the tense voice, but he wanted Karen to hear.

"I am here, Mother," he said aloud but under the music, hiding in it. "I'm here."

He was still saying it when the needle slid into the silent space and then bumped against the label. He waited, listening to the empty rhythm of the thumping needle, for her to come.

"You're ruining that," Karen said, coming in to take the needle off. She studied the dials to find the cutoff switch.

"The one on this end," Kevin said, not getting up. His dark frame seemed sunk in the rumpled bed, and he put his free hand over his cast. Karen sat down on the edge of the bed and put her hand on his leg, her light fingers on the shinbone. She rubbed gently for a moment across the fine dark hair there and then drew her hand away.

"So," she began.

He was silent, waiting for her. He thought to himself that she hadn't arrived yet. This was not his mother but some ghostly apparition of her wearing white slacks, a pale peach blouse, bracelets jangling from her slender wrist. She touched her hand to her cheek, pushing back a loose lock of slick auburn hair that slipped there. It was a familiar gesture, an unnecessary, habitual one. He wanted to pull her hand away and see the curve of the wayward hair over her eye; he wanted to see her hidden behind it, her eyes averted with shame at what she had done to him.

And would do again. She would leave him again. He felt how temporary she was, her thin body barely resting now on the edge of his bed while he was chained down, inert and stifled, separated from any reasonable existence. She fingered an earring beneath her hair, then lowered her hand to her neck, index finger straight up and over her closed lips as she looked at him thoughtfully.

"Does your arm bother you?" she asked finally, worrying him with her eyes. He always thought people saw through him, but Karen seemed not to see him at all. Her eyes were on his cast.

"No."

"But you miss tennis and swimming?"

"Of course I do." He felt himself crumbling, soul bared and awaiting her invasion.

"Well, it won't be too long now," she said, smiling. She rested her hand on his knee. He felt a slight reflexive jerk, but she didn't seem to notice.

"Well," she said again, moving her hand and getting up. "I'm going to stay in a motel while I'm here so I'd better call and get a room."

He couldn't let her go. There was nothing he had ever wanted like he wanted her in his room. No matter how ephemeral she was, he would always feel empty without her, and so he sprang instinctively into action, grasping at this unlikely chance to keep her.

"No," he said jumping out of bed. He caught her by the arm so that they faced each other. He was taller than she.

Just that fact startled him a little and then brought him quick assurance. He could persuade her to take his room.

"I'll sleep on the sofa downstairs. It makes a bed. You can take my room."

"I couldn't possibly do that, Kevin," Karen said, moving back from him.

He followed her, tracking close at her heels. "Of course you can. It's a good enough bed, and I won't bother you. There's nothing here I need except a change of clothes now and then."

"What about your dad, Kevin? What about Tom?"

"He'll be all right. Sure, he took your getting a divorce kind of hard at first, but he's all right about it now. He's probably expecting you to stay. I know Wren is."

"Well." Karen searched his face for a moment, then put out her hand to touch his cheek. "If it's all right with everyone else," she said.

"Good. I'll change the sheets right now, then I'll clear out. What else do you need?" He moved away from her touch. He felt so good inside, so sure of himself now that he'd convinced her. He didn't think he'd ever influenced her before, and so, gathering his dirty laundry in his good arm, he thought that this might just mean a new beginning for them. His exuberance finally burst through his face so he was standing there grinning foolishly at her.

"Don't do a thing, you hear? I'll strip the bed, get your bag, buy you roses. I'll do everything!"

When all was done, he wanted to invite Melanie for dinner. Bliss thought it was a mistake, but he was so happy she didn't have the heart to deny him. Besides, having dinner guests might lessen the strain on Tom. They wouldn't have to talk about anything important with the children there. So Bliss told Wren she could invite someone, too, and Wren asked Jolene.

They gathered in the living room at six-thirty, Karen looking perfect and fresh in print dress and sandals. She seemed so adaptable, proving to them she could for a few hours play the parent, wife, daughter-in-law, as easily as she could turn her interest in other directions. Now she wore an alternate face, both spirited and relaxed, that could woo them into believing this was just the kind of evening she'd been longing for.

Bliss stood in the entry to the dining room watching how she leaned on the arm of Kevin's chair, her hand on his shoulder. She's leading him on, Bliss thought helplessly, and she doesn't even know it.

Kevin felt her presence, her thigh pressing against his cast. Without looking up, he knew how beautiful she looked, how she twisted her head slightly to laugh as if she must lean away from any overt emotion, how her fingers played on the back of the chair almost in his hair.

Melanie was on the sofa between Wren and Jolene. She had planted herself in what seemed like the safest place, wedged in away from Karen's questioning grasp.

"What do you do?" the woman had already asked Jolene, as if she'd expected a fourteen-year-old to have exciting summer employment and a day worth talking about. Jolene was used to Karen, and so she'd joked about being in bed till noon, watering the plants, having to vacuum the cushions on the family-room sofa even though it was her sister's boyfriend, not hers, who'd spilled peanut shells all over the place.

Karen had laughed as if she enjoyed Jolene's dramatic descriptions of such mundane events. Life on another planet. Melanie expected to be tongue-tied when her time came, if it ever did. She didn't want to be drawn out, exposed to this woman's friendly yet critical scrutiny. She felt so alone, even though she was perspiring between Wren and Jolene, dug in as tight as a tick.

She shut her eyes for a moment, not wanting to see how far away Kevin was, and opened them to see Mrs. Jackson, who waited in the doorway for a lull in Jolene's chatter so that she could call them to dinner. Melanie hoped she was sitting at the far end of the table, maybe next to Kevin's grandfather, who was smiling magnanimously at her from time to time, as if he sympathized with her discomfort. As long as she wasn't beside either of Kevin's parents she could manage all right. She certainly had less than nothing to say to Mr. Jackson, although he seemed harmless enough sitting there in an armchair and looking a little detached from the conversation, as if he weren't interested or didn't mind his wife having the show. What could he do about it anyway? Well, how should she know what he thought about anything?

All she knew was that some of the Jacksons were crazy. Her mother had told her that, not in a gossipy way, but just letting the truth be known. Her parents didn't hold it against Kevin. Melanie was sure of that, although she knew they hoped her going with him didn't become more involved than it already was. Sometimes she wished that herself. Sometimes she truly didn't know what to do with Kevin. He could be so impatient and moody. He got angry over absolutely nothing and then acted carefree just as fast.

Chapter Fifteen

Well, he wasn't the only person to run hot and cold. Sometimes she was that way herself, no matter how she tried to control it. Of course, she did manage somehow. After all, you have to go out in public. You have to be civil to people. Kevin didn't seem to know that. Sometimes he wasn't even civil to her.

She watched his mother's hand on his shoulder. It wasn't just the ring she was wearing, a big blue stone that might be a real sapphire, that made the hand look foreign but also the way the fingers rested, touching just enough to make a person shiver. Melanie had seen Karen's picture, and still she hadn't been prepared for someone like this. Why, there was nobody in town like her. Nobody who could be, no matter how hard they tried. That was the really neat thing about her. Being like she was seemed so natural to her. There wasn't an act in it at all, unless her snuggling up to Kevin like she'd been doing was an act. And Melanie didn't think so. She was just showing him she loved him, that was all. And he needed a year's worth of hugging. She knew that.

Bliss called them to dinner, directing Melanie to Bill's left, Wren next to her. Kevin and Karen on the opposite side. Jolene and Tom with her. That would work. Gave everybody someone they could talk to.

"Let's hear about your new job," Jolene said while they were passing the serving bowls around the table.

"I don't know very much about it yet," Karen said lightly. "At least not much that isn't a trade secret. I've found an apartment, though. The company is leasing me something in the building they own. I flew up to see it last week so that I could decide which of my things would work

167

in it, and it's lovely. Very high up and roomy. A wonderful view."

"So," Tom said slowly from the other side of the table. "It's settled. You're going." He spoke as if he thought some response were expected of him.

"You know it's settled," Karen said, smiling at all of them. "This time next month, I'll be in Chicago."

Melanie looked at Kevin. She wished she were next to him, holding his hand under the table, pressing comfort into his palm like a fortune he could believe in. She saw his altered expression, the quick sinking around his mouth, eyes lowered as if there were no one at the table he could look at.

He had thought he could keep her. Melanie saw that in his face. Saw how the excitement of the afternoon, his frantic preparation of the room, his jubilant phone call inviting her to meet his mother, had failed him. She stared at him hard while the conversation continued around them.

You have me, she said to him as spoon clicked on china, salt and pepper passed from hand to hand. You have me.

Chapter 16

He was absolutely livid. Anger boiled up in him, rattled in his head, made him crash his battered cast into the steering wheel.

"Kevin, stop it!" Melanie screamed. She was trying to avoid his flailing arms and get to his face. Her hands on his face would make him stop.

But he struck out at her, a glancing blow that skimmed her cheek and shoulder to land with a dull thud on the back of the seat. She gave up, turning away from him with her hand on the door handle for a quick escape. The dark slugged in on her through the open window, a steamy rancid night coming off the river in hot, puffy breaths. Where could she go? There was a car parked farther down. She could see its solid gray form against the dark trees, but she didn't recognize it. Anyway, out there was probably no better than in here. She released the handle and turned back toward the front while Kevin sobbed beside her, his forehead on the rim of the wheel, arms crossed over his head.

"What's wrong with me?" he begged her. "Just tell me what's wrong with me." ·

"Nothing, Kevin. There's nothing wrong with you." She

wanted to put her hand out to him but she knew that this close to diffusing his anger, he would turn to her, expecting her to give in. So she let her hands stay in her lap, fingers still as if she were calm inside. "I just don't know what you want from me, that's all. I mean, I can't figure you out, Kevin."

"Join the club," Kevin said. He pulled out his handkerchief, blew his nose in it, then turned to face her, his face worn down, flat with exhaustion. "I just want to be close to you, Mel. I just want us to really be together. I know we've talked about holding off. I mean, I know neither of us are ready to get married or anything, but what the hell, Melanie, the way everything is going, I need somebody right now. I need to know you're with me. Can't you see that?"

She saw. The months spun past her as if she were looking at a movie screen. She watched those first tentative moments of intimacy between them, the initiation rites of soft new kisses, fingers sliding against flesh. She saw how so very little had once been enough. She closed her eyes.

"I can't do it," she said quietly. "Not like this, when you're so angry. I'm scared, Kevin."

"Then you don't love me," he said.

"You can't say that."

"I need you, Melanie."

She could hear the crying in his voice although he held steady, forcing anger to combat his grief.

"You think I'm sick, don't you? You think there's something wrong with me. Well, maybe there is. I feel crazy. That's the truth. Maybe I am."

She felt such pain for him. He was as heavy on her as he'd

be if she were locked under him. "Let's go somewhere else, Kevin. Let's ride around and get some air."

He waited a moment for her to change her mind, but she didn't move until he turned the ignition key. Then she put her hand over the edge of his cast, entwining her fingers in his. He shifted into reverse and pulled away from the river with her hand still locked in his. On the open road back into town he felt her getting ready to speak. He chewed on his lip, waiting.

"Kevin," she said, "maybe we shouldn't see each other for a few days. You're going to be busy with your mother here and I'm tied up with those kids every day. Maybe in a week or two . . ."

A few days. She meant forever. He knew she did. He turned the corner onto her street.

"I don't have to be home yet," she said, releasing his fingers.

"I think you'd better," he said. He couldn't believe how calm he was. This felt a lot like breaking his arm. He'd known it was broken, and so it was too late to fight it. He'd just had to go with it. This was like that. He felt as though Melanie had already left.

He stopped the car in front of her house but left it running.

"I'll call you in a few days," Melanie said softly. "Or you call me. Will you, Kevin?"

"Sure." He didn't look at her.

"I love you, Kevin. You know that, don't you?"

"Sure."

Her lips brushed against his cheek. It was all he could do to stay still.

"I'll see you then," she said, warm breath against his ear.

"Yeah." He held the brake and pushed on the accelerator at the same time. The car raced anxiously.

"Well, 'bye."

He didn't watch her go. Before she was halfway up the walk, he had gunned the car away from the curb, roaring off into the dark where no one could find him.

Early the next morning, Sam called Wren to tell her he had a ride into town.

"Come meet Mother and Daddy," Wren said.

"I thought we could do something fun," Sam protested.

"Fifteen minutes with them, I promise that's all. Then we can go somewhere for a little while. Not long, though, because Mom's just here for a few days and I want to be with her all I can."

"Okay. See you in thirty minutes."

He was there in time for breakfast. Bliss set another place at the table in the kitchen and spooned him out a serving of scrambled eggs. "That's fine, Mrs. Jackson," he said. "I had cereal a couple of hours ago."

"Hours ago?" Tom said. "What time do you get up, boy?"

"About five-thirty in the summer. I do the feeding before we get into the field. Today we're just cleaning out the packhouse, so Daddy gave me the morning off."

"Do you work every day?" Karen asked.

"No, ma'am. Not most Saturdays and never on Sunday."

Karen laughed, her voice sweeping over their heads while Sam ducked his head and worried a toast crumb with his fork. Here she was, a guest in her in-laws' house, divorced from her husband who looked drugged to him, visiting her children who she saw only a few times a year, and she didn't seem at all embarrassed or apologetic.

"You remember Sam's folks, don't you, Karen?" Tom asked. That was what Bliss and Wren were always asking him. *You remember, don't you, Dad?* "John and Kathryn Holland," he continued slowly, checking his memory as he went. "They live out near Collins Crossroads in a big old farmhouse where John grew up."

Sam could see her tracing lines of memory into her past, but she came up blank. "Of course I do," she said. "Sam, do give my regards to your parents."

"Thank you, I will." Sam looked at Wren, who was smiling back at him. He was a success. Her smile drew him into the family circle, knighted him with her approval. "And thanks for the breakfast, Mrs. Jackson."

"We're going out for a little while," Wren said. "Would you like to come with us, Mom?"

"Thanks, sweetheart, but I'll stay here and visit with your dad. Maybe Kevin will get up before noon and join us." She waved them off with her hand, a kiss blowing from her fingertips.

They went to the playground at Larkwood Elementary because there were few places available to them at nine in the morning. The air was still and dusty around the swings, and so they jumped on, pushing with their legs until they were skimming the air above the dust, catching the breeze in their faces.

"What do you think of her?" Wren called to Sam as they passed each other.

"Who?"

"Mother, of course. What do you think?"

He knew he could give the sort of answer Wren expected, easy phrases slipping off his tongue; but he bit down on them, looking instead for what he really felt about her mother. He knew she made him uncomfortable. Not apprehensive exactly, just wary, as if she had discounted him already. Maybe she thought he and Wren were too young to really care about each other, but he suspected she hadn't even thought that far. She hadn't taken him seriously enough to think about him at all.

But he did care about Wren. He was fifteen, the same age his dad had been when he'd first seen Kathryn Lassiter and told her, just three days later, that someday he would marry her. Sometimes he thought he could say that to Wren. He wanted to. He had imagined the possibility of it, had even spoken of it, while they danced at the Candlelight Inn but Wren hadn't thought he was serious. He hadn't even known it himself. Then gradually, as he'd come to trust how he felt about her he'd seen that Wren wasn't like Kathryn, and so he'd held back, protecting both of them from the possibility of Wren's rejecting him before he'd had a chance to let time work for him.

Now he knew why he'd hesitated, licking back words so often ready to spill. This morning had showed him why. Wren was like her mother. Someday, she would be just that beautiful. She would be that confident, too, that determined. He could see now that Wren's seriousness about her music wasn't a passing fancy, a childish dream. She had come to ambition naturally, instinctively, and now here was someone—her own mother—to show her how ambition could be used.

"What—do—you—think?" Wren was shouting on the wind.

"I think she's wonderful!" Sam called back, gripping the swing chain hard as he watched Wren fly past him, out of reach.

From where he lay on the sofa, Kevin could hear their voices in the kitchen. He hadn't bothered to pull the sofa out last night, and so he pressed his face into the back of the seat and pulled the blanket across the side of his face, blocking out sound. He could hear his mother anyway. Her light laughter pounced on him, her voice snaked into his ear. He heard the collecting of dishes, the short spray of water rinsing away their scraps, the chewing growl of the garbage disposal.

He swung off the sofa, pulling the blanket around him, and went upstairs to shower and dress before Karen had time to come up. He didn't want her to see him looking hung-over, the stench of beer on his breath and clothes, his face puffy and stained from crying. He had bawled his eyes out. He remembered that, the crying and drinking he'd done simultaneously while parked behind a beer joint off the highway, a six-pack on the seat beside him. He didn't even know how he'd gotten home. Habit. The car knows the way to carry the drunk, as to grandmother's house we go.

He got clean clothes out of his room, noticing for a moment his mother's things spread about on his dresser. Her jewelry carelessly dropped there, pots of cream and eye makeup cluttering his clean spaces. Her shoes were on the floor, one of them turned on its side as if she'd kicked it off.

Her blouse flung over his desk chair. They all seemed right to him, like perfect accessories to his own austerity.

He stood under the hot spray, spewing out water, lathering his hair, rubbing fat white blobs of shampoo on his chest. He turned his back to the jet and let the fine hot prickles shower down on his tense shoulders, washing away the miserable night. The water calmed him, and he took in deep cleansing breaths of steamy air. He had been standing there several minutes before he realized his cast was soaking wet. It would have to be changed.

He watched the saw chew into the plaster, then the spongy gauze coming loose. His arm was white, thin, not conceivable as an appendage of his. He looked at the soft lifeless wrist on the table and wanted to strike it, pound it back into hot circulation, make it burn and sting and itch. But he was afraid. It was the same fear that had stopped him from turning his bike into the side of the car and kept him from tightening his lips around a thin joint of grass. Whatever he did to himself would be worse than he'd intended, an impulsive moment mushrooming into endless hours of regret.

The new cast was lighter, smaller, and smelled starchy. He liked the cool, damp feel of it. It was so clean. Looking down at it, he wondered why he'd been so ashamed of the other cast since he'd always wanted a definable injury like this, something his mother would have to acknowledge but not blame him for. He wondered how he'd managed all these years without a cast, an acceptable symbol of his broken self. Why shouldn't he use this broken arm then, turn it to his advantage? That was what successful people did, wasn't it? Use their disadvantages just like they did their advantages. It didn't matter that Melanie was gone because he still had a chance with his mother. He hadn't lost yet.

He felt better. Holding his cast aloft to help it dry, he smiled at the receptionist on the way out and when a carload of his classmates passed him on the street, honking and shouting, he waved his good arm after them, fingers spread in a victory salute.

She was lying on his bed wearing a sundress, bright green with a border of yellow and white daisies. It was a dress to go out in.

"You're bored," Kevin said, looking at the cover of the magazine on her stomach.

"I'm not," Karen said. "It's nice not having to go somewhere every minute. I absolutely never have a day like this."

She patted the bed, and Kevin sat down facing her.

"You have a new cast," she said.

"Yes. Getting it wet was so stupid. I just didn't think."

"No harm done." Karen smiled. "This one looks better."

"It's lighter and smaller." He held up his arm so she could see that his fingers were freer now.

She hardly noticed; her attention was already somewhere else. Back in Atlanta, he gathered. Or speeding ahead to Chicago.

"I hope you can come see the new apartment sometime, Kevin."

He was right. Chicago.

"At Thanksgiving. You and Wren can fly up and spend the holidays. I'll even cook a turkey." She laughed and threw back her arms against the headboard. "Well, actually

I'll order one. We'll have a catered Thanksgiving dinner. Something to tell your friends about."

"I don't have any friends," Kevin said. He looked away from her. If he saw her face, he wouldn't be able to get out the words he wanted to say. "I broke up with Melanie," he continued. "Well, it's no big deal. It's been coming for a long time. I just got fed up, you know."

"You'll find another girl friend," Karen said lightly.

He could tell she didn't understand what was coming. He wanted to prepare her.

"So that's over and I'm at loose ends."

Her hands came down into her lap, fingered the cover of the magazine. He watched the hands, the slight, almost unperceivable fluttering above the glossy paper.

"I want to live with you, Mom," he said. "I want to come to Chicago now."

She had, how long, five seconds? How long did it take to say yes? He would give her that long. Time to envision him in the roomy apartment, high up and with a view. Time even to put out her arms to him. He watched the fingers tightening on the edge of the magazine. She gripped it as if she were about to swat an insect, eliminate some pesky interference. Still he waited.

Time ran slowly, running out. He looked at her, eyes tearing. His vision was curiously blurred at the edges, but her face was clear to him, as solid and contained as marble.

"All right," she said, but it was too late. She had hesitated. All the willingness in the world wouldn't change that. All the pleading she might do, all the entreaties she could muster, wouldn't make those empty seconds go away.

"No," he said, getting up. He couldn't look at her, and

so, his back to the bed where she still lay smiling up at him, he made his stumbling way to the door. "I was just kidding," he said, facing the hall. "See you later."

He went down the steps, through the hall, and into the kitchen. It was almost noon. He would go to the store. He had promised his grandfather he'd put in a few hours this afternoon. He felt himself contracting, pulling inward where everything mattered but nothing showed. He had been wrong. The cast on his arm was just that, a splint for a bone, and nothing more.

He hadn't understood. He'd been stupid. Made every mistake in the book. He'd trusted other people. Now he knew better. He had learned a lifetime of lessons in two lousy days; from now on, he would trust only himself.

Chapter 17

That evening, after dinner, he played Hearts with Karen and his grandparents while Tom and Wren sat at the piano. Tom picked out tunes in his head and Wren added the bass notes so that they made a cheerful, happy noise, laughing together when they invented a particularly wretched combination.

"That's it," Bliss said, tallying the score at the end of a hand. "Let's have some iced tea before we go to bed."

"I think I'll take a walk," Kevin said, sliding back from the card table. "How about it, Wren? Wanta go around the block?"

"Sure," Wren said, a little surprised at the invitation. Kevin hadn't wanted to walk anywhere for six months, not since he got his driver's license.

The night was cool, bringing rain toward them from the west. The sky blew darkly and they watched the constant movement of the treetops in the yards as they passed.

"Are you all right, Kevin?" Wren said when they were on a different street. "Did something happen between you and Melanie?"

"We just aren't going to see each other for a few days."
Kevin held his cast to his body. "I don't think Melanie likes
Mom very much."

"I don't believe you," Wren said and then was quiet. If
their mother wasn't the real reason, she knew Kevin didn't
want her to know it.

"She thinks I'm crazy," Kevin said finally. "Sometimes I
think I'm crazy, too."

"That's crazy!" Wren giggled and hugged his free arm to
her side. "Honestly, Kevin, I know Melanie likes you a lot.
You'll get back together."

"I'm just not planning on it," Kevin said. "And it's
okay, Wren. I can handle it. That's sort of why I wanted us
to come out like this—to tell you I can handle whatever
comes along."

"Like what?" Wren wanted to joke with him, but she felt
strained. His seriousness pulled her down, made laughter
seem frivolous.

"Like Mom's going to Chicago. Things like that."

"Her going to Chicago doesn't change anything for us. I
thought it would, but now I see it doesn't," Wren said.
"And Daddy—he's better, Kevin. I know he is. He was
down at his office today, going through files, and he's called
Mrs. James about coming back to work part-time for him. I
know he's had bad days, he'll always have bad days, but I
think he's doing just fine, Kevin. We're lucky. You know
that, don't you? We really are."

"I guess so." Kevin stopped on the walk. "Let's go back
before it rains," he said. Big drops smacked the leaves above
their heads.

"Kevin," Wren said, following him home, "the way

we've always wanted things—I don't think they will ever be like that." She caught up and latched her arm through his. "But no matter what happens, we have each other."

"Yeah," Kevin said, and at the front door he hugged her hard.

He lay on the sofa in his clothes, the Seconals in his pocket. A handful of them in a clear plastic bottle off his grandfather's shelf. Upstairs a toilet flushed, a door snapped shut. He could hear the rain spanking the windows. It sounded distant, like little slaps through thick padding. Storm windows, storm doors, kept him safe. Fiberglass insulated the walls and roof, kept cold and heat out. Bolts dropped. The steady hum of air conditioning overrode natural sounds, the honking of car horns, the murmurings of bugs, the night's wings on the walls.

He was alone in the dark. No light glinted on the wall of trophies across the room. The television set was a black hole, denser than the other dark. He would sleep a little while, just until they were all asleep upstairs. It was all right to sleep a little. A trial run. He closed his eyes, his fingers tight against the plastic bottle in his pocket. He felt sure he could do it.

He awoke to hear the mantel clock in the living room chime three. The rain had stopped and the house was still, no thumping and bumping goblins about to bother him. He got up and went to the kitchen. The light inside the refrigerator didn't come on. That was when he realized the electricity was off. He poured a glass of milk in the dark, his finger inside the rim of the glass to tell himself when. He felt so efficient, competent to manage in the black quiet like he was doing.

He walked cautiously back into the family room, holding the glass of milk close to his chest, and found the sofa with his foot. He sat down and spilled the capsules into his hand. He felt them on his fingers. He could almost see their red glint in the darkness. He pressed his full palm to his mouth, sucked them in, swallowing hard on the milk. It was so easy. Already he felt something like comfort.

Bliss awoke a few minutes before four, although she had to look at Bill's pocket watch to know for sure. The moment she awoke she knew the electric clock was wrong, its numbers glowing dully at two-thirty. The surge of power back into the house was what had caused her to lurch in her bed and fling one arm out toward Bill's back.

She ran her fingers down his spine over the soft worn cloth of his pajamas. Touching him should make her feel all right, but it didn't. She waited a minute or two, listening to the house. All was quiet, and yet she felt restless, her nerves pinching slightly across her shoulders, her temples beginning to throb. She got up and went down the hall to Tom's room.

He was sleeping peacefully, his face toward her. He was truly better; these two difficult days with Karen in the house were proof of that. She was proud of him. She started back to bed and then paused in front of Kevin's room, remembering that she hadn't told him a proper good night. She did worry about him. More than she wanted Karen to know, more than she wanted to admit to herself, although she knew there was nothing she could do to prevent the problems he must face. Sometimes she wanted to hold him, though, proof of her constant care. She wanted to touch him when she knew he was most apt to draw back, on a night like this when his parents were in the house and he was alone on a makeshift bed, separate from them in all the ways that mattered to him.

She turned and went down the hall, lifting her gown on the stairs, feet moving quickly now, as if she felt an urgency like a live current loose in the air. The family room was dark, trapped in the natural stillness of night, and yet she felt anxious, her chest suddenly clammy as she felt her way to the sofa like a blind woman. She put out her hand to find his shape, a foot uncovered, a hand loose. She touched a shoulder. Her hand skimmed his shirt sleeve, down to his elbow, over the cast to his fingers. He was so still, so unyielding under her frantic touch. She lifted his hand into hers and felt a slick cold capsule drop into her palm. She was screaming when she reached for the light.

He didn't want to see anyone. Why couldn't they understand that? He lay in the semidarkness of a hospital room waiting for night while dim light skimmed the white sheets on his bed and hung dully on the bottle dripping its clear liquid into his vein. Bringing him back to life.

He closed his eyes but could feel the nurse in the room, a practical, diligent figure adjusting the drapes, slipping the dusky afternoon out of his view. He could hardly believe it was the afternoon of the next day, fifteen hours of unconsciousness between his grandmother's scream and this moment when the nurse's voice came over him again, sliding in like the curtains easing together: "Your folks want to see you."

He opened his mouth, felt cool air rushing down into his burning throat. He swallowed down on the air because it was a solid thing, like a bite of food swelling on his tongue. He began to gag, pushing on the air, forcing it past a weird burning obstruction in his mouth.

"You're all right," the nurse said, coming to take his head. He leaned over her arm to retch into the pan, but nothing came. The glob of air sank into his stomach. "It's from the tube, honey," the nurse said. "You're just about raw inside from getting pumped out. Lord, getting saved is hard."

Now he could see she was an old woman with firm arms and hands made strong from lifting bodies, turning mattresses, wheeling beds. She leaned him back on the pillow where he twisted his head from side to side, dripping sudden sweat.

"I'll tell you the truth, honey. There's some anxious folks out there—they're loved ones, you can tell that. Been sitting there ever since I came on, and from the looks of them, they were here a long time before that." She wiped across his face with a soft wet cloth, holding his trembling chin in her hand as if he were a child. "Be still now. Let's get you looking better. You're probably going to look better than they do."

"I can't," Kevin whispered. The words hurt him.

"Can't what? Can't see those folks? Of course you can. There's no doctor here to say otherwise. You ought to see them, too, just for a minute. Let them see you're fine so they can go home and get some rest. Then you can get some rest, too." She pumped up the blood pressure cuff, released it slowly, watching the gauge while she listened to his blood rush on, thwarting his intentions.

"Not all of them, then," Kevin said. "Just my grandmother and my sister. Just them."

"I'll get them." The nurse patted his hand and left him alone.

He could see the night in their haggard faces, the long, weary day when he'd been comatose, even the frantic hour when Bill had pressed his mouth to his, nose squeezed shut, keeping him alive until the rescue squad squealed into the driveway to pour portable oxygen into his lungs, the needle into his wrist. Pumping out. Pumping in. Keeping him.

Bliss took his hand, lifting it away from him. He thought she was touching a severed arm because he felt nothing except a flowing regret in his bowels, a rumbling sadness in his singed throat. How could he have done this to her? It seemed so unreasonable, so demented. But, then, he must be insane. A lunatic, although he'd felt so sure carrying the pills in his pocket. Even swallowing them, he'd not wavered from his plan of escape from the life they'd forced on him. Melanie and his mother would be sorry.

But now it was Wren who came to his other side, the bandaged side, and put wet, trembling lips briefly to his cheek, as if she feared her touch would do him harm. They stood silently beside his bed, watching him, their bodies barricading him against any memory of hurt. He released tight fingers from the sheet and held out his hand to Wren so that both of them were touching him now, holding on.

"I'm sorry," he said. "I'm so sorry. I didn't know it would be like this."

Chapter Seventeen

"We know, Kevin," Bliss said. "You're all right now. Just rest. Sleep."

He couldn't help but sleep. He felt their fingers releasing him, although he wanted them to stay with him. He wished he could tighten his fingers, pulling their hands back into his, but he didn't have the strength. He felt his eyes failing and fought against their slow closing. It was no use, and so he gave up, seeing in the moist, furry space between his lids that they were still there.

In the car on their way home, Bill put his arms about Bliss, drawing her close. She let him hold her, relinquishing herself to the comfort of his familiar embrace. They took up only half the seat, and so Wren had the rest, although she wanted to be between them. She felt like an outsider without Kevin. She should have stayed with him over everyone's protest. She belonged more with him than here.

Karen was driving. She whipped the bulky Cadillac around corners and slid under changing lights, taking them home. Beside her, Tom slouched toward the door, the side of his head against the glass. Karen had her window down, and the wind, warm and humid with her scent, blew across the seat into Wren's face. She closed her eyes against blurry, windy vision, then opened them again. In the dark she had doubted where she was, where they were going. Nothing seemed real.

Karen knew the way, her sense of direction unimpaired although there were new one-way streets to take her by surprise and construction to disrupt her memory. She spun the wheel with one hand, anxious to get them there. She didn't want to look at the family, their faces heavy with guilt. Soon their stunned grief would turn to questions. Why would he do such a thing? What had they done so terribly wrong? How could they have loved him and yet failed him so miserably? She knew the answers already. The accusing finger would inevitably point at her, as if she were not, even now, bent low with punishment.

In the driveway she idled the car, waiting for them to get out. They were slow, hesitant to appear at the scene of the crime, even though it was her crime, not theirs. She raced the motor to hurry them along.

"Aren't you coming in?" Bliss asked her through the window. Tom was moving slowly, like a sick person, toward the house with Wren at his arm.

"I'll be back soon," Karen said, looking at the house. The windshield blurred the sunlight through its smears. "I'll switch cars."

"No need," Bliss said. "Take mine." She stepped back to let Karen go.

Karen drove downtown, waited patiently this time in lines of traffic at lights, slowed to let pedestrians jaywalk, stopped on caution. The town looked the same to her although there were new storefronts, a recent addition to the bank, a modern post office. The changes seemed insignificant compared to the change in herself.

Seventeen years ago she'd come here, diploma tucked away, wedding ring where an inexpensive opal had been. She had done all the right things at first, penance for having eloped with Tom Jackson, and then had appeared on Bliss' doorstep, invading their comfortable style with her less-than-perfect credentials. All those years ago, she had done what was expected, had made herself fit in. It had even been what she truly wanted.

Now no one seemed to recognize her. No one waved or chased her down for news about Kevin. No one knew yet. At least that sin, that omission, was still secret, locked in her chest.

She turned out of the business district, going toward Bliss' because she saw there was no place else to go. It was a circuitous route she took, winding down residential streets until finally she was on the street where she and Tom had lived together, where she had brought Kevin at three days old intending to be incredible in her care, to protect him forever. She passed the house without even recognizing it.

Bliss had called Mr. Kensley. The next morning, before visiting hours, he came in jeans and T-shirt, whipping out his minister's pass when the nurse gave him a critical, suspicious look.

"The privileges of power," he said, pulling up a chair next to the bed. He leaned back, hands in pockets, thumbs out. "Feel lousy, huh?"

"Guess so." Kevin studied the liquid dripping down the tube.

"I had one of those once. Had my appendix out. Hated the thing. Felt like a vegetable getting irrigated."

"I don't mind," Kevin said. "It's something to be attached to."

"That's what we've got, buddy. A wired-up, strung-out generation. So how long do we have to meet like this?"

"I can go home tomorrow."

"You want to?"

"I guess so. This room costs a lot of money and I'm not sick or anything."

"Exactly what are you, Kevin? I assume you've been thinking about that."

"Crazy."

"Uh-huh. No way. Packing some powerful artillery, maybe. Expecting to get shot down, maybe. But crazy you're not."

"A psychiatrist came yesterday," Kevin said.

"Diagnosis?"

"He didn't offer one. I guess I did the talking."

"You told him you were crazy?"

"No, I was saving that."

"He asked you why you did it?"

"Yeah."

"You tell him?"

"No."

"You want to tell me?"

"It seemed like the best thing to do."

"What were your other possibilities? I'm just curious."

"Just get along, I guess. Without Melanie. Without Mother. Everybody's taking off. I thought I might as well go, too."

"But they could come back. Did you plan on coming back?"

"I didn't think about it. I thought I was doing the right thing, the best thing for everybody."

"Do you still think that?"

"I guess not."

"Why's that?"

"Because I feel like an idiot. That's worse than being crazy."

"Do you want to see a doctor for a while, just till you're sure you're not crazy? Or you could see me. I've had some therapy experience. I'd be willing if you are. I guess you know you're not going to get out of this without seeing somebody."

"You're not going to talk religion?"

"Not unless it just naturally comes up. Sometimes it does, you know."

"You're not going to get me praying and all that. I'm not into that."

"I'll try to keep God out of it."

"Okay."

"Okay what?"

"Okay, I'll talk to you."

"In a couple of days then. I'll call you if you don't call me. After you have that cast off, maybe we'll go somewhere. Out in the country on the bike. Want to do that?"

"Sounds okay."

"I'll see you then."

The nurse was watering his plant, something yellow in a pot Karen had sent that could be planted later in Bliss' garden. She had wanted to brighten up his room.

"What's the matter?" the nurse asked him, seeing his face in the mirror.

He tightened his lips, grimacing against a loud sob that roared up his throat. He shut his eyes tight and, in the self-inflicted dark, looked back into the nightmare he had created, his mind racing, still searching for release.

"Why did he do it?" Bliss asked Mr. Kensley. They were sitting in the living room, perched on the edges of the chairs as they waited.

Jack Kensley looked at them: Wren, scratching a bite on her arm, picking nervously at the enflamed skin; the mother, looking lovely with the pale, grieved look of a person recovering; the father, leaning forward as if ready to pounce on any glimmer of hope, healthier than Kensley had expected him to be although he certainly didn't look well; the grandparents, hands touching, waiting.

"I'm sure we'll discover an accumulation of reasons," he said slowly. "But the specific and immediate ones he expressed had to do with Melanie Washburn and"—he nodded toward Karen—"with you, Mrs. Jackson."

"He and Melanie stopped seeing each other a couple of days ago," Wren said. "He told me the night he did it. You remember, Grandmother, we went for a walk together. He said it was just temporary, and he was very calm about it. Hardly upset at all."

"And me?" Karen asked. She held her body still, posed as if she were about to be photographed. "What did he say about me?"

"Just that you were leaving him."

"But he knew that," Bliss said. "He's known that for some time."

"It's something else," Karen said. She slumped a little, hands curling in her lap. "He asked to come to Chicago with me. He wanted to live with me. I told him he could, but then he said no, he didn't really want to. He said he was only kidding."

"And you believed him?" Wren pressed her fists into her cheeks. Blood pounded in her temples. "How could you, Mother? Don't you know us at all?"

"Wren!" It was Tom who sprang toward her, catching the twisting, angry arms. "Wren, be still." He pressed her to his chest. "Don't blame your mother," he said into her hair. "I'm responsible, too. Neither of us has been what he needed."

"But you couldn't help it, Daddy," Wren sobbed.

"That doesn't change what I've done to Kevin."

"The important thing is to decide what to do, how to handle things when he comes home," Bliss said.

"Treat him as normally as you can. I think he'll be embarrassed, even ashamed of the worry he's given you, especially you and Mr. Jackson. He'll want to make amends, I think. Let him. Let him feel he has as much control over living as he wanted to have over dying."

"I'll take him with me. I want to," Karen said. She brushed her hand over her face, removing a glint of tears.

"That's a possibility," Mr. Kensley said, "if he wants to go. He'll probably need time to make that decision. To come to terms with whatever the situation is with Melanie, too. You'll have to help him be patient. His body is recovering quickly, but his spirit will have to heal as well. That's a slow process."

They went their separate ways. Tom to the sun porch where the white furniture gleamed in the moonlight and the night hugged the screen. Bliss and Bill to their bedroom, shutting the door behind them as if to lock out grief and find solace in each other. Karen to Kevin's room where she sat on the edge of his narrow bed, head dropped toward her knees, shoulders heaving forward as she spilled out slow, soundless sobs.

Wren went to the piano and sat before the keyboard, waiting for a melody to come, something she wanted to play that hovered in the back of her head behind the clutter of the past two days. Finally her hands went to the keys, discovered there a C-sharp chord. Put a G-sharp to it. Heard the opening bar of the *Moonlight Sonata* lingering on the pedal. She started again, the notes cool on her fingers as if she were touching flowers.

What had Sam said to her? You play so well, you can teach music and play the organ? Words that made her skeptical of him, as if he could alter her ambition, make her less or at least different from who she intended to be, just by loving her.

She had been wrong. Loving Sam was what would make everything right. She wouldn't be like Karen, giving up husband and children for a career. She wouldn't abandon infants, expecting them to love her anyway, in spite of all the emptiness she left. She would hold on to Sam and let her mother go. That was what she would do.

Chapter 18

Jack Kensley sat in Kevin's room, blond head catching window light. The first thing he'd done was to open the curtains, forcing Kevin to see his visitor and the room in definite, unavoidable shapes. Kevin blinked against the sudden brightness, but he didn't complain. It wasn't worth complaining about.

"So," Kensley said, "your mother didn't want you to go to Chicago."

"Who told you?"

"She did. She said you asked, she said yes, you said no. Is that how it happened?"

"If that's what she said."

"What do you say?"

"I don't remember the exact words."

"What about the exact feelings, Kevin? What were you feeling?"

"I don't know."

"What about now? How do you feel now? What's it like to be a statistic?"

"I don't think I need this," Kevin said. He wanted to

swing off the bed, get away, but moving took too much effort.

"It's either me or a guy with a couch. I come to you, what more do you want? You think I haven't failed at something? You think you're the only guy that screwed up?"

"I don't think I'm the only anything."

"That's good. That's real good. Because you're just like the rest of us, Kevin. You feel stupid, right? You already told me that. But I happen to think failing at suicide is better than succeeding, if you know what I mean."

"If I'd made it, we wouldn't have anything to talk about," Kevin said. It was hard not to smile. He didn't want to feel anything, much less pleasure at their fencing. That was what this was—some sort of fencing. It wasn't so bad.

"Little humor there, huh?" Kensley said.

"Hardly."

"Actually, you feel as bad now as you did then, right? I mean, what's changed? Melanie is still out of the picture, your mother's still going to Chicago. Nothing's changed except that you've exposed yourself."

"They tiptoe around me," Kevin said.

"They're scared. They don't trust themselves."

"They don't trust me, either."

"What about that? Are you trustworthy? You don't feel any different, you said that yourself."

"When I did it, I thought it was the only solution. It was like I was taking a test and there was only one answer. No multiple choice."

"And now? Do you feel different about that?"

"I don't know exactly. I guess it doesn't seem like the only answer anymore."

"That's good."

After Kensley left, the light was still bright in Kevin's room.

Bob Seger and The Silver Bullet Band sailed against the wind, pushed around the jamb, stretched out into the hall to pull Melanie toward their sound. She stopped at Kevin's door, took a deep breath, and rapped twice.

He didn't hear her. She rapped again, her knuckles crunching on the wood.

"Yeah?"

He was on the bed, arm free of the cast but in a sling that held it stationary against his chest. The music was loud, crushing her. It kept her out, and so she went to the turntable and lifted the needle, then clicked off the current.

"Got something against Seger, huh?" Kevin said, motioning toward his desk chair, which had been turned around for visitors. Jack Kensley had sat there just an hour ago.

Now Melanie sat down and settled her purse in her lap. She wished she'd worn jeans instead of this sundress. She felt foolish, as if she'd come to a party on the wrong night or had ordered veal when everybody else was having burgers.

"Seger's all right," she said. "I guess you've been wondering where I've been. Well, I've been busy. Really busy." She was trying to look at him, but it was hard. Her eyes kept pulling away. "Keeping my cousin's kids, you know. Helping around the house. I went to see that new

Redford movie Friday, though, the one about prison. It's gross, really gross. But you should go see it. You'd probably like it."

"People who try to kill themselves probably like gross things," Kevin said. He fingered his sling, touched the fracture gently.

"I didn't mean that, Kevin. You know I didn't."

"I'm being hard on you, Mel, because you're getting ready to be hard on me. I can tell. I've got this sense about it, you know. The way a dog can feel an earthquake or something."

"I just came to see you, that's all. I've been wanting to. I called over here all the time to find out how you were."

"And how was I? Okay? Fair to middlin'? A basket case, ready for the funny farm?"

"I called several times, and they said you were doing just fine." Melanie looked at the wall above Kevin's head. There was a movie poster from *King Kong* on it. Gorilla with woman in hand.

"I never thought you'd do anything like this, Kevin. I never thought you were——" Melanie stopped before she said what she'd been thinking. He really was crazy.

"Yeah, well, neither did I. It just sort of happened." He wanted to tell her he'd never do it again, but he knew saying that wouldn't make any difference. He felt strange with her in his room. It wasn't right for her to see him so closely, in such an intimate place, when it was all over between them.

"Well, I told you I'd call you in a couple of days. Or you could call me," Melanie said. "I guess that's what my coming today is all about. Keeping a promise."

"I guess we'll see each other when school starts," Kevin

said. "I mean, we'll probably have classes together and all that."

"I hope so, Kevin. I want us to always be friends." Melanie stood up, uncurling her purse from her lap. She smoothed her skirt. "Well, I'm glad you're doing so well."

"I'm fine."

"I see you are. Well, 'bye." She slipped to the door as if she were sneaking away.

" 'Bye."

He tried to relax on the bed, let his body melt into its cushioned surface. He felt wet all over, tears washing down his face, hanging on his lip, slipping to his neck. He turned his head into the pillow, arm tight to his aching chest, and let the sobs come.

"Did you think about how Wren's life would be changed when you took the pills, Kevin?" Kensley leaned back in the chair, his feet on Kevin's bed. Kevin was staring at the ceiling.

"I guess I thought she'd be all right."

"But you wanted to hurt somebody, didn't you?"

"Not Wren. Melanie, I guess. And Mother. I already told you that."

"But you thought you'd be here to see the effect, didn't you? You didn't really think about what being dead is, did you?"

"I guess not." Kevin slid up on the pillows so that he was looking at Kensley. "I just felt so alone. My parents control my life, you know, but it's long distance. I live with other people because of them. Everything's the way it is because of them."

"So now they're to blame for whatever goes wrong? Your broken arm, mediocre grades, losing Melanie, the normal everyday trauma of getting past sixteen?"

"I thought I shouldn't blame myself for everything," Kevin said, a smile playing on his voice.

"*Touché.*"

Kevin studied Kensley's face. It was a friendly, open face. He wished he looked like that.

"When I was a kid," Kevin said, "I used to plan accidents, little plots to bring Mother back, but I could never go through with them. I was too afraid. I guess taking the pills was my big try."

"And you intended to go through with it, didn't you?"

"Yes." He paused and looked away from Kensley. "The current went off that night," he continued suddenly, as if he were just now remembering it clearly. "Did you know that? I took the pills in the dark, so pitch black I couldn't see what I was doing. I didn't even know how many I was taking. I couldn't see anything, but I knew that if I could see, I wouldn't recognize anything. Nothing seemed real.

"I had felt absolutely alone all that day. Detached. In a way I felt okay being alone like that. I felt I deserved it. I had control over it, too. Wren and I went for a walk. I was so calm. I've never been so sure about anything. It seemed so reasonable, so sane. It was the first time in months I hadn't felt a little bit crazy."

He could see Kensley was going to let him keep on talking.

"Sometimes when I think about it, I don't believe it was me that did it because I can't remember very much about it. It doesn't feel like me. I can't remember actually taking the pills, what it felt like. Stealing from my grandfather—that was the hardest part—but once that was done, it was like I had already taken them. I got cold, I remember that much. I remember when I shut my eyes, it wasn't any darker behind my eyelids than it was in the room. I tried to open my eyes again, just to make sure, but I couldn't. I didn't really even want to." He waited, expecting Kensley to say something. "Do you think Granddaddy will let me work in the store again?"

"You'll have to ask him. What about your mother, Kevin? What are you going to do about her?"

"I can't think about her yet." But when Kensley left, his mother was all he could think about.

Karen came from the motel where she'd moved the day Kevin came home from the hospital. Tom had tried to give her their old room, but she'd refused and Bliss had let her. Wren didn't even offer her space.

Kevin was at his desk, writing a thank-you note for flowers he'd been sent, when she came up the stairs to his room, knocked once, and opened the door. He looked up to see she was wearing what looked like a new dress, something flowery and cool, as delicate as an evening dress. He went back to the note, his weak fingers cramping around his pen as he formed careful letters like a child just learning to write.

"I'll do that for you," Karen said, watching him struggle through his name.

"No," he said. "Grandmother already offered, and I told her I wanted to do it. It'll help me get strength back in my fingers." He put the pen down and turned away from his desk. "What do you want?" He motioned toward the bed and she sat down on it, near the edge. Balancing.

He remembered how she'd looked lying there a week ago, relaxed. Content, he'd thought. That was where thinking got him.

"I want to talk to you, Kevin." The tone was ominously practiced.

"I'm listening."

"I want you to come to Chicago with me. Live with me next year."

So. He had won. A smile tried to ease across his mouth, but instead he forced a frown, fingering the note he'd left on the desk and studying his shaky signature. *Kevin Jackson,* he had written. That was his name. An identity that separated him from every other living creature on the earth. Even from her.

"I don't think I can do that," he said slowly, although he could imagine himself there, could see them making late suppers together, him doing homework while she did needlepoint or studied window layouts; could see her kissing him at the bus stop when he went off to school or on the opposite end of the tennis court after he'd taught her to play, matching him stroke for stroke.

It was impossible. Of all the possibilities of his life, this was the impossible one. They would always be the odd couple, bickering for space, time, affection. Give me. No, you give me.

"I'll see you on holidays," he said, speeding up a little. Why take all day to tell the truth? "Wren and I'll come at Thanksgiving for that catered turkey."

"You're sure, Kevin? You're really sure?" Karen was

looking at him. He felt her eyes holding him together.

"I'm sure. And, Mom, don't worry. I'll be all right now. I promise."

He meant it. They were words he'd mumbled in the direction of Jack Kensley, of Bliss, of Wren. But he'd never been really sure. Now he was. He wanted life however he could get it.

"I never meant to hurt you, Kevin."

He put out his arms to her. He could feel the strain of his injury, the sore muscles of his arm stretching, but nothing could stop him from reaching out to her. Nothing ever would again, and yet from now on he would always know that what he reached for was momentary, transient, inaccessible, and made all the more precious by its elusiveness.

Chapter 19

Karen invited Wren to spend the day with her shopping, swimming in the motel pool, then an early dinner. She was leaving the next day. Another week in Atlanta and then the grueling move to Chicago, the unpacking, long hours of orientation into the job. She wanted this last quiet, easy day alone with her daughter.

Wren didn't want to go. She could hear Bliss in the kitchen clearing away after breakfast, and she longed to drop the receiver and run into those arms, arms that had always been there, that would deny her nothing, not even an excuse. But she couldn't ask that of Bliss, and so she turned her mouth into the speaker and said on a heavy breath, "Okay."

Karen barely heard. "I'll pick you up around eleven then," she said. "We'll have a light lunch somewhere and visit some shops. Don't forget your swimsuit."

They hung up; Karen slowly, her hand lingering on the receiver as if the conversation didn't seem quite over to her, while Wren snapped the button down and up, listened for the dial tone, and then touched the digits that brought Kathryn Holland's voice whirling into her ear.

"Is Sam there? It's Wren."

"He's on his way out, honey, but I'll try to catch him."
Then the voice. "Wren?"

"Sam."

"Wren, what is it? Are you okay?"

"I just wanted to tell you I may not be here tonight. I'm spending the day with Mother and we're going out for dinner. It's her last day."

"Oh."

"Sam?"

"I'm here."

"I know you are." She paused. "Well, that's all I wanted."

"Listen, Wren, call me when you get home."

"I'll try to. I can hardly believe tomorrow she'll be gone," Wren said suddenly.

"She'll be back, Wren."

"But it won't be the same, not ever again."

"Maybe it will be better. Think about that."

"My birthday's soon. The next time I see her, I'll be half a year older. She won't even know me."

"She doesn't know you now, Wren."

"Who does?"

"I do."

"What do you know?"

"I know I love you."

"She loves me, too."

"I'm not competing with her."

"I know. I didn't mean that."

"Yes you did. If I thought I could beat her out, I'd run all the way into town."

"Tomorrow she'll be gone."

"She'll never be gone."

"You're jealous."

"I just wish I could spend the day with you."

"You can. On the Fourth."

"Call me tonight. I'll be here."

"I know."

The sounds of the town took on a breezy quality, reflecting her mother's light laugh, the tinkling tune of her bracelets when she reached for a dress on a shop rack, the soft *ah-h-h* that escaped when she saw Wren in something she especially liked—a sundress of bright yellow trimmed in white, a soft straw hat pressing her curls to her forehead and cheeks. It was like being in another place, where charm came naturally to everyone—the waiter at lunch, who returned time after time to fill their water goblets and recommended a light kiwi fruit dessert; the clerk in the jewelry store, who lay out chain after chain on her velvet square until Karen had seen them all and had selected a fine serpentine one with a delicate heart-shaped locket that lay just inside the neckline of Wren's shirt.

"Happy birthday, sweetheart," Karen said and kissed her there in the store while the clerk patiently lay the other chains back inside the case.

Wren fingered the locket, still cool on her skin. She had thought Karen was looking for something for herself, but now she saw the purpose of the day—it was to celebrate her birthday two weeks away.

"Can't you stay until then? Or come back?" Wren asked, caught in this moment of excitement.

"You know I can't," Karen said. She touched the locket, her fingers grazing Wren's throat. "I'm never here on the right day, am I?"

"No."

"I remember the day you were born so clearly, Wren. People say you forget the pain and they're right, but you remember other things so vividly. A certain look, some offhand comment that is caught in your memory because your senses are so keen at that moment, so ready to devour everything. I remember there in the delivery room, the doctor told me you were going to be a pianist because you had such long, narrow fingers. He probably said that to half the mothers. It was something nice to say. But I remember it, not so much because your grandmother's family is so talented as because he was confirming something I already knew to be true. You could be someone special. I knew you could do something marvelous, something extraordinary. I willed that on you the moment you were born."

"Shall I wrap that?" the clerk asked.

"She'll wear it, thank you," Karen said and moved away from Wren to write the check.

Wren wanted to follow her. Words jumped in her head, confusion bumping against the truth. Perhaps Karen had willed it, but Bliss had seen to it.

Bliss had held her at the piano when she was three, patiently repeating a tune. Bliss had explained, day after day, the strange markings on the staff; she had counted slowly, clapping her hands softly at Wren's shoulder. Bliss had sat through the beginner and elementary books, had listened to variation after variation, had bought more music, explained symbols, taught theory, reminded her to listen to herself. She had taught her what the sound should be like.

And then, two years ago, she had found another teacher, someone who perhaps knew more and who certainly cost more, and had given up an afternoon every week to drive Wren to her lesson at the college. And then had continued to listen, to correct practice mistakes, to console and praise.

Bliss had done all that, and yet her mother had been there first. Wren had seen photographs of herself, an infant in those arms that now embraced her shoulder, jewelry jangling. She had seen a younger, fuller face looking down at her, had felt soft, colorless lips on her toes, her fingers, her tight full baby stomach. She had been inside that body, had been attached, connected to that will. You will be, the pulsing cord had said to her. I am making you, linking you to me forever because we are closer than you will ever be to anyone. I am your first dream, your first memory, your first pain.

Outside the heat was stifling, and they hurried to the car and headed for the motel pool. Karen lay in the sun, her skin glistening with oil, while Wren swam, dipping in and out of the water, watching the sparkles underneath and stray wisps of clouds above. Once when she surfaced, Karen was at the edge of the pool, dipping her hands into the water and dripping it on her arms.

"You should come in," Wren said, hoping she would.

"I'd rather get the sun while I can," Karen said. "We'll have to dress for dinner soon. I want to get you home in time to say good-bye to Kevin and your dad."

"And grandmother."

"Of course, your grandmother. And your grandfather. I

care about them a great deal, Wren. Surely you know that. I could never have done what I have if it weren't for them."

"I guess not." Wren dog-paddled away and then ducked into the water. When she came up, Karen had gone back to her lounge chair and was stretched out on her back, eyes closed to the sun.

At dinner, they were both quiet. The room was almost dark, although it was still light outside. White candlelight trembled on the table as Wren nibbled at her salad. Even after the swim, she didn't feel hungry.

"I think Kevin will be all right," Karen said finally.

Wren nodded.

"And you? What about you? Will you be all right?" Karen reached across the table to catch Wren's hand.

"Yes."

"Growing up isn't all that easy. I think I got married to avoid it."

"Was that the only reason?"

"Of course not. I loved your father. I wanted children."

"And then one day, you didn't?"

"No, Wren. It was never like that. I just couldn't manage it all. At first I didn't know why I was dissatisfied—it's still impossible to explain because I had a good husband, two beautiful children, a nice home. But slowly I realized I was more than a little discontent. Even before Tom was sick, I felt it. I suppose that feeling had always been there. It was as though I was misplaced and had to keep looking for myself.

"I didn't have a discernible talent when I was a girl, not like you do. I could draw a little and knew what looked well; I recognized style. I suppose I had a natural sort of taste, an instinct, but I didn't have any experience or any place to use that ability. I just knew I wanted to have a life that was uniquely mine. When I realized I could have a career, I was flabbergasted, completely unstrung with excitement. I didn't realize what it would mean. I didn't know what I'd have to give up. It was as if there were two roads and one of them looked so familiar, so ordinary. I just had to take the other one. I had to."

"What if it hadn't worked out?" Wren asked. She rubbed her finger against the sweating glass.

"If I hadn't been successful? I suppose I would have come home and tried to be an adequate wife and mother. I don't think I could have ever been more than adquate, though."

"We wouldn't have minded," Wren said.

"Perhaps not." Karen sighed. "I don't deny I've been selfish, Wren. But if I say I'm sorry and don't come back here to live with you and Kevin, being sorry doesn't count for much, does it?"

Wren was silent, fingering the glass.

"We have to live with things the way they are, not the way we want them to be."

"But things are the way you want them to be," Wren said bluntly.

"So I can't win, can I?" Karen said lightly. "I didn't want us to argue, Wren. I thought you were old enough now for us to talk. I've been waiting for a chance to say these things to you. You're growing up. You have your music, your friends, and now Sam. Before you know it, you'll have to be making decisions about your life, the kind of decisions I didn't know how to make. I probably shouldn't have married. I probably shouldn't have had children. But I did.

I'm glad I did. I know you can't believe this, but I have bad days, days when I can't get my work done and I go home feeling lonely and aggravated, and I'm so grateful that I have you and Kevin. You're the only connection I have anymore, the only steadying factors. And yet, I wouldn't change my life. Can you understand that?"

Wren studied her uneaten dinner, afraid to look up. She didn't want to see that sun-touched face, colored now in candlelight, the slender fingers, glossy nails toying with a spoon, the luminous eyes holding her own face captive in its unyielding light.

Back at home she could fall into Bliss' arms or lie across Kevin's bed with him, listening to music that could take them both away, flooding their brains with acoustical comfort. She could pick up the phone and have Sam tell her how they would spend the Fourth of July at the town fair, hear him paint her future as bright as the flags that would flutter above their heads. She could have almost everything.

"I understand," she said to her mother, and looked up to see Karen pass her finger beneath her eye, lifting away a tear. "We should go so that you can say good-bye to Kevin."

"I know," Karen said, forcing a smile. "I dread it."

"He won't make it hard," Wren said.

"I know he won't intentionally, but it will be hard anyway."

They moved away from the table. In the motel lobby a family was checking in. Children scampered around the potted trees and fell giggling over the back of the sofa, releasing their cooped-up energy after a long drive. While her husband filled out the registration form, the mother watched them indulgently. In her arms she held a sleeping child, a girl of less than two, still baby-plump, her fine curling hair damp against her mother's arm, her body relaxed, almost dangling in that safety.

"Oh look," Karen said softly. "Look at her."

But Wren could not.

Chapter 20

Jack Kensley took Kevin seventy-five miles up into the foothills where a lake lay locked within a rocky boundary. The bike, smelling of oily exhaust, was hot under them, but the wind in their clothes was clean, burned through with afternoon sunlight. Kevin held on to the backrest, his shoulders pulled back, his weak wrist straining against his gripping fingers. They were carrying a cold-pack with two steaks in it, frozen pancake mix for breakfast, canned soft drinks, and orange juice. Two bedrolls, insect spray, enough money for a motel room in case it rained.

Jack followed a forested highway into a state park and then up a bike trail, while Kevin leaned back on the metal rest as Jack's weight shifted toward him. Jack was wearing the shiny jacket with which the town now identified him, and the slick ballooning fabric grazed Kevin's chest and helmet. He wished he could take his helmet off to feel the wind and the jacket's cool surface. He didn't feel he needed protection beyond Jack Kensley's practiced skill with the motorcycle.

He was sweating under the helmet, and he thought he might go swimming when they got there. He could feel himself weightless in the cold, dark water. There were deep pools between the rocks, places to dive straight into it with elbows tight, head catching water. Then go deeper until his lungs were stinging, hard and full in his chest. He would have to come up, flash pale arms above the warmer, sparkling surface and then lie on his back, exhausted, watching the sky between the moving shadows of the trees.

They were there. Jack stopped the bike. Kevin slipped off his helmet, pulled himself off the bike, staggered on bandy legs, and then stretched, twisting his sore wrist above his head.

"Arm hurt?" Jack asked.

"No. Just stiff." Kevin swung his arms and did a few knee bends.

"We've got a couple of hours of daylight left. Wanta swim?"

Kevin was kicking off his boots. "You coming in?"

"Yeah, since we don't have a Jacuzzi."

Kevin stripped down to his shorts. "I brought swimming trunks, but they're in the bedroll."

"There's nobody here but us," Jack said, sliding out of his jeans and then his underwear.

Kevin stepped out of his shorts and slid down a smooth slanted rock into the water. He went under, pushing himself down. It was cold and deep. If he wanted to, he could stay down there. He surfaced, lifting his head back and whipping water from his eyes to see Jack Kensley looking down at him.

"You can dive from there," he called, watching the arms go up, torso arching forward. The body knifed the air, broke the water with a sudden jet of spray and came up close to him, treading.

He felt the proximity of the body, arms sweeping just beneath the surface. He was surprised at how strong this man was, and he felt vaguely leery of him when just minutes ago he'd felt so trusting. He had been caught up in the passing scenery on the bike, feeling safe even as menacing cars hung close and the sun-struck pavement glinted just feet away. He'd felt safe even with the speed. But now they were still, water pressing on all their surfaces, lapping into their mouths and licking their ears, shriveling them.

"Great dive," Kevin said, spitting water.

"College swimming team," Jack said. "Ten years ago I was hot stuff."

"You've still got form," Kevin said, floating on his back. His head felt light, but his body was still cold.

"I think we're a lot alike," Jack said. He ducked under the water and then shook his hair back. "I've just got ten years on you. Ten years from now you'll probably be married, started on a career, settling in, thinking about having kids. You'll be contributing to the community."

"Don't plan on it."

"You're the one who's got to plan on it," Jack said. "I'm just telling you it can happen. Of course you can stay single, move to Paris, pump gas, play the bongos, settle in Alaska. You can do anything, be anything."

"Is this the official pep talk?" Kevin asked and then swam away, toward shore.

"No," Jack called after him. "Do you need one? '

Kevin climbed up on the rock and lay back, letting the sun dry him. In a few minutes, he felt Jack beside him.

"Once, when Wren and I were little . . ." His eyes were still shut but he knew the man was there, listening. "The first or second time Dad got sick—the doctor told Grandmother in front of us that Dad should never have gotten married or had children. He couldn't handle responsibility, the doctor said, and he looked at us. I don't suppose he meant that we were the cause exactly, not us as specific people, but I always felt we were. Wren and I both did—still do, I guess." He put his arm over his eyes.

"Do you think you made your father sick?" Jack asked quietly. "Do you really think that?"

"Sometimes I do—most of the time, I guess. But sometimes I think he would have been like he is no matter what anyone did. Something would have gotten to him. Sometimes I think it doesn't matter what anybody does or doesn't do. Last week he was talking about getting into the insurance business again. He was going down to the office. He even called his old secretary, and she said she'd come back part-time. But yesterday he came home early in the afternoon and went to sleep. He didn't get up until this morning."

"Maybe he didn't feel well."

"No. It was probably Mother's leaving. That and her getting the divorce. Add what I did to his other problems, and he drops out."

"So you're to blame again?"

"I suppose so." Kevin sat up, looking away from Jack. "I'm getting dressed."

"You're going to have to ditch that guilt you're lugging

around," Jack squinted up at him. "I don't see how you carry it from one day to the next. Why don't you bury a little of it, Kevin? What good is it, anyway? Something a stupid doctor said when you were eight. Just get rid of it."

Kevin looked back at Kensley stretched out on the rock. The distance between them seemed enormous, a giant step. He pulled his shirt over his head, wondering why he'd thought this man would really understand. All those hours they'd spent in his bedroom, on Kevin's turf, much of it bantering, idle talk, but more than he'd said to anyone in years, even to Melanie. He had thought he could go on talking, seeing how Kensley was willing to listen without much advice or opinions. He had been like an anonymous ear perfectly tuned, but now Kevin saw the ear had a body attached, a strong body that had felt the stress of hard exercise and mental work, had loved a woman. Jack Kensley wasn't some kid you could spout off to and not have it make any difference. What this man thought counted, what he questioned needed answers. Kevin slipped into his shorts and pulled on his jeans. Still Kensley lay on the smooth rock, face to the sun.

"I'm going up the trail a little ways," Kevin called down to him.

"Gotcha!" Jack called back, not moving.

Kevin moved slowly along the darkening trail, the leaves above him turning gray in the evening light, the ground obscured in shadows. He was surprised Kensley was letting him wander off alone. He had felt so watched lately, everybody wanting to know what he was doing, where he was going, protecting him from himself. Protecting themselves, too. Showing interest, searching for topics of conversation that might interest him, avoiding mention of Melanie, of school, of his hazardous return to the living.

Only Kensley wanted to know about these things, and yet he was the one person willing to let him go. Kevin stopped on the trail, seeing ahead a glimpse of space, the afternoon sky above the water. He could drown himself, hang himself by his belt. He could have a second pill bottle in his pocket. Kensley knew all that, but he also knew Kevin wouldn't do it. He understood without saying so that craziness didn't necessarily repeat itself. Sometimes a moment of madness was the cure. Kevin turned back toward their campsite. It didn't seem very far away.

They grilled the steaks over a fire Jack had built between two rocks, held thick slices of bread over the coals to toast them, ate fruit cocktail out of snap-off cans for dessert. The trees wrapped them in night; the cold dark smell off the lake invaded their camp light, clung damply to the rocks and grass.

"Wren used to be afraid of the dark," Kevin said into the night. "She wanted a lamp on in the hall. You can see it from outside, just this faint light through the upstairs center window. If I come home and can't see it, I always get irritated, even panicky sometimes. I always want somebody to remember to turn it on."

"I guess we all want things to stay the same. Except ourselves, of course. We expect to change, but we don't like for anyone to complain or be critical of us for it." The voice came from beyond the fire, a sleepy, restful voice.

"What I dread most is going back to school. Everybody will know about it."

"You won't have that problem if you give people

something else to think about you," Jack said. "Something like your being one of the best tennis players in the school. You could get active in the athletic club. Find something else to join. By Christmas you'll be dating again. People aren't going to spend all that much time thinking about this summer unless you give them reason to."

"It's definitely over with Melanie," Kevin said. He thought he might start crying. He couldn't think about school without her.

"Maybe so," Jack said. "But not many people end up spending their lives with their first steady. It's a good thing, too."

Kevin could hear him settling in his sleeping bag. A spark jumped in the ashes, touched the ground, and died there.

"Jack," he said, "I think I'm going to be all right."

"So do I, Kevin."

He lay hearing the night in the trees above him. The sound swept low, touching the water, swelling softly again into the leaves. It was the wind moving, and it carried him to sleep.

Chapter 21

The high school athletic club was sponsoring the dunking booth at the town's Fourth of July celebration. Sam called Wren to ask her to talk Kevin into helping out.

"We've got people from the football, basketball, baseball, and wrestling teams. He could represent the tennis team. Ask him, Wren."

"I'll ask, but he probably won't do it. He hasn't been anywhere but camping with Mr. Kensley. He hasn't even been to the store."

"That can't go on forever, can it? The carnival's a good place to start. Everybody'll be having a good time. Ask him."

He agreed. "Thirty minutes getting dunked, that's all I'll do," Kevin said.

"An hour," Wren said. "Nobody's going to get a hit anyway. It's a lot of girls trying to knock down the guys."

"Well, I know something about that."

"Oh, Kevin, don't get smart, just do it."

"I'll do it, I'll do it," he groaned, throwing up his hands in mock defeat.

So they went to the fair in the town park where a

traveling carnival had parked its trucks and vans along the edges and set up rides in the open space. Club booths had been arranged during the night on the perimeter—groups selling crafts, fudge wrapped in cellophane, hot dogs, and drinks. There was a booth for taking instant pictures, bottles to knock down, dishes to flip pennies into, an airgun for blasting at a moving row of chipped, faded ducks.

"A bunch of junk," Kevin said, following Wren and Sam between the flapping canvases to find the dunking booth.

"You don't have to stay past your hour," Wren said to him.

"Thirty minutes."

Wren sighed and hurried after Sam. "He's in a terrible mood," she whispered over his shoulder.

"We'll take him home with us this afternoon for the picnic," Sam said.

"I don't think he'll go."

"Mom called your grandparents. The whole family's coming."

"You're kidding!"

"Would I kid you?"

"Here it is."

The basketball coach was inside the booth working on the drop mechanism. "Hello," he said. "Finally somebody shows up. This thing is supposed to get started in fifteen minutes, and nobody's here but me. Half the football team promised to be here at ten o'clock, but I don't think any of them have learned to tell time yet. Get in here, Kevin, and give me a hand. Better yet, throw something at that thing and let's see if this lever is functional."

Kevin slammed the baseball into the target, and the seat over the water tank gave way.

"It's working!" the coach said. "Now, who's first on the schedule?"

"I'll collect the money the first hour," Sam said.

"Why don't you get dunked and I'll collect the money?" Kevin asked.

"Because nobody wants to knock me down, dummy. I bet the entire tennis team from Westhaven is coming over here to get you."

"Go on and be first, Kevin," Wren said. "At least not many people are here yet."

But within thirty minutes, the park had come to life. Children tugged at skirts, pulling their mothers along from ice cream stand to carousel, from miniature train to portable horror house. Groups of young people gathered at the central ticket booth, buying a three-for-a-dollar special that lasted until one o'clock. The churchwomen from the booths wandered around, examining the wares in other booths, getting ideas for next year. The hired carnival workers settled into the rhythm of their work, punching tickets, locking bars into place, fastening chain gates, easing gears into action. They watched lethargically as the rides circled and spun, listening beneath the frantic screams and laughter to hear the familiar, constant chugging noise their machines made.

Jolene appeared wearing shorts and a snug cotton shirt. She smelled of suntan lotion and the candy apple she was biting into, the red syrup staining her mouth and dripping onto her chin.

"I just love these things," she said, chewing a bite of yellow apple. "Want some?"

"No thanks," Wren said. "I was just going back to the dunking booth. Sam's over there."

"I'll come with you," Jolene said. "Who's that getting dunked?" she asked, the apple wobbling on the stick as she took another bite.

"Kevin."

"You're kidding!"

"No. I didn't think he'd come, but here he is."

"I'm going to do it. I'm going to dunk him if it takes all day and every cent I've got," Jolene said happily.

"Jolene!"

But Jolene was racing across the grounds. She dropped the half-eaten apple in a trash can and dug a dollar bill out of her pocket.

"Oh no, it's Jolene," Sam said, faking a pain in his chest. "Kevin, it's Jolene!"

"She can't do it anyway," Kevin called from the cage where he sat suspended over the water tank. "Jolene, you're wasting your money!"

"Well, it's for a good cause," Jolene answered. "Three tries for a dollar, right?"

"Right," Kevin said. "You've got fifteen minutes, Jolene. Because I'm getting down from here in fifteen minutes."

"You're getting down sooner than that," Jolene said and reared back to pitch the first ball. It slid off her fingers, falling short of the target.

"How much money have you got?" Kevin called to her.

"Enough," Jolene said. "Now you better keep your

mouth shut so you don't drown in there!"

A crowd was gathering, people nudging each other, grinning while they waited for the spill.

Jolene threw the second ball which glanced off the target, perfectly aimed but not hard enough.

"That girl's going to do it," a man next to Wren said. "She's determined."

Jolene lay in her third pitch, and the ball sailed into the target as if it were exploding. The latch disconnected under the force of the hit and as the seat dropped, Kevin disappeared into the tank of sloshing water. He had taken a deep breath, preparing himself to stay under, and so he held himself down against the side of the tank.

"Oh God, he's drowned!" Jolene wailed. "Sam, get him out of there!"

The crowd stirred, waiting. Wren looked nervously at Sam, hoping he'd know what to do. Sam watched the tank. He could see Kevin's head below the murky surface. Suddenly the face appeared, shaking back water and grinning at them.

"You scared me to death!" Jolene screamed at him. "I swear, Kevin Jackson, that was the meanest thing you've ever done!"

The crowd relaxed, chuckling, but still waited to see what would happen.

Kevin was reattaching the seat. Then he pulled himself back on it.

"I'm going to do it again, Kevin Jackson," Jolene said. "You're going to wish you'd stayed down there all day."

"Jolene," Kevin said, swinging his legs above the water, "you want to go to the Hollands' picnic this afternoon?"

Chapter Twenty-one

Jolene clutched the dollar she was about to lay in Sam's hand and looked at Wren. "Am I invited?" she asked.

"I think you're being invited right now," Wren said.

"Are you inviting me?" Jolene said to Kevin, her voice considerably softer.

"I guess so. I mean, you've got to eat, don't you?"

"Your time's up, Kevin," the basketball coach said. "I've got somebody to take your place up there."

"You're not joking, are you, Kevin?" Jolene asked.

"Jolene, would I joke with you?"

"Would he?" Jolene asked Wren.

"I don't think so."

"I'll go, I'll go," Jolene said. She looked at the crumpled bill in her hand and pushed it back into her pocket.

Kevin climbed off the seat and slipped out of the back of the booth and into the coach's van where he'd left his clothes. So he had done it, exposed himself. Taken a risk. It hadn't been so hard. He rubbed down with a towel and slipped into his clothes, then stood in front of a small mirror to comb his hair. The face he saw looked different, the mouth lines somehow softer, the eyes more direct. It was a receptive face, ready for sunlight. At least he wouldn't scare anybody with it. For once he didn't even scare himself.

Tom refused to go to the picnic. He lay on his bed, head flat so that Bliss had to come all the way in and look down at him to see his face. A sunken expression, flesh lax. No blood flow there. Face shut off, dead to her.

"You must get up, Tom," she said, touching his shoulder.

He opened his eyes, lids heavy, half closed against the pressure of even so diffused a light. "Go without me."

"I can't, Tom. We won't. We'll stay home if you don't come. Please try to get up, Tom. You know John and Kathryn Holland. You like them. We won't stay long." What could she say to convince him, except the truth? "Tom, if you stay here, it will be even harder tomorrow. You can't give in like this, not so soon. Think about Wren and Kevin."

"I can't," he whispered. His lips barely moved.

She wanted to strike him, lay solid slaps against that spongy flesh, dig fingers to the bone, ripping him loose. But she held her hands together against his chest, feeling all her muscles tightening, little spasms shooting across her shoulders, a knot of tension in her temple. She couldn't do it again, couldn't face the drive to the hospital, the careful words, the temptation to do him harm. She could never make up for what he had lost or give him what wasn't hers to give.

"Please, Tom," she said. "Do this for me."

"I can't. I'm sick, Mother."

"You have to try," she said stonily, turning her face away. She could hear firecrackers down the street, someone laughing in the next yard.

"I can't go anywhere," he said, turning slowly away from her.

"Then we'll go without you." She went to the door, determined not to look at him again, but in the doorway she turned back, unable to leave without taking this image of anguish with her. Her lost child.

At the Hollands, Kevin and Jolene sat on the edge of the porch, their feet and legs dangling in the sun. "Look at Janice Barker," Jolene said, nudging Kevin into attention.

"What about her?"

"She's hanging all over Paul, don't you see that?"

Kevin squinted at the girl who was wrapping ears of corn in foil. "She's not even touching him," he said. "Besides, why should you care?"

"I don't," Jolene said. "I just notice things like that. I mean, I can tell you her intentions."

"Her intentions? About what? She's wrapping corn, Jolene. There's nothing else to it."

"Don't you believe it. She's planning something. That's what girls do, get interested in domestic stuff like that. She's acting like she's the hostess."

"You're crazy, Jolene. You know that? You really are."

"You wanta sing, Kevin?" Jolene nodded toward Wren who was playing her guitar at the other end of the porch.

"No, but you go ahead and join them."

"I'll stay with you," Jolene said. "It's too hot to sing anyway."

A breeze came across the yard, bringing charcoal smoke with it.

"Listen, Jolene," Kevin began. He was pressing his fingers into the flesh of his newly healed arm, checking it against new injury, assuring himself. "Listen, this is a family picnic, you know. I mean, it's just people getting together."

"I know that." Jolene gave him a sideways glance and then hugged the porch post next to her, pulling away from him. "You want me to know this isn't a date or anything like that, don't you?"

"Well," Kevin said, putting his hand on her shoulder. The seam of her shirt ridged under his fingers, and he ran his hand up it to her neck so that it rested, palm below her ear, where she was warm and tense. "You're family, Jolene. We're practically related. Anyway, I think I'm too old for you."

"You are not!" Jolene blurted, almost pulling away from his hand; but she was suddenly still, not willing to relinquish his touch. "The older people get, the less age matters. I mean the difference between being five and ten is not exactly the same as between twenty-five and thirty, is it?"

"I guess not, but I'm still not dating a freshman. You understand that, don't you? I just didn't want you to get the wrong idea about my asking you out here today. It just seemed right that you should come, that's all."

His fingers fell away from her neck, and she shivered. "You're not over Melanie, are you?" she asked softly.

"I guess not."

"But someday you will be."

"That's what everybody says."

"Someday I'll be sixteen and you'll be eighteen," Jolene said.

"Eventually."

"Not eventually," Jolene said. "In less than two years."

"That's a long time." Kevin was grinning at her.

"Not when you've waited fourteen years already," Jolene said.

Bliss and Bill left the young people at the farm and went home to see about Tom. Bliss had kept the light burning in the hall and it shone through the window as Bill unlocked the door, letting her in. She went straight up the stairs, along the dim hall to Tom's dark room. He was asleep, and so she and Bill stood there as if they were reliving a scene of long ago when they would come in from an evening out and watch their sleeping baby for a while, holding each other in the dark. Between them, there once had been a fluttering, easy joy that he was safe and well. Now they embraced again in the dark, a groping touch as if they had forgotten where hands and arms went, how a head bent into a shoulder.

"Tomorrow he'll be better," Bill said softly, his hand against her hot trembling cheek.

"No, I don't think so," Bliss said, her voice thick with longing.

The air around them had an aged, dank smell, and the contours of the room, as familiar as their own, seemed peculiar and alien. They went out into the hall, closing the door behind them. They moved down the passageway to the room where they would lie in wait for their other children to come home. They went silently because there was nothing left to say.

Chapter 22

Wren had played straight through *The Songs of Oscar Hammerstein* and was now in the Baptist *Hymnal,* stumbling around in the flats. She had started her morning practice with the assigned piece, a Chopin polonaise, but her fingers had been stiff and inept even after fifteen minutes of exercises, so she'd abandoned the difficult fingering to try to relax with something fun. Nothing worked. Even her shoulders felt rigid; she rolled them forward, then backward, stretching as she played.

"Lousy morning, huh?" Kevin said from the doorway where he'd been watching her. He was wearing his tennis clothes although the doctor hadn't said he could play. He swung the racket, working his wrist.

"Are you supposed to be doing that?" Wren asked, giving up in the middle of "Blessed Assurance."

"I could ask you the same thing," Kevin said, coming in. "What happened to Chopin? To Beethoven? To Schumann and Liszt?"

"They are being spared," Wren said.

"You're not giving them the old heave-ho, are you?" He

sat down on the bench next to her and fingered an awkward scale with his left hand.

"Some days I just get tired, that's all. And when I'm tired, I start wondering why I have to be so damn serious when other people aren't." Wren put her right hand on the keys, resting them lightly above a chord, but she didn't strike.

"Nobody says you've got to do this," Kevin said, dropping his hand.

"I say I do."

"And what about Sam?"

"Haven't asked him." She struck the chord, grimacing. "When I'm with Sam, I'm thinking about other things."

"Got it bad, huh? I know what that's like. When Melanie and I first started dating, I wanted to be with her every minute. I had to drag myself to the tennis court. Sometimes I just dragged myself as far as her house. I admit to weakness of the flesh." He wasn't laughing. "But"—he thumped the keys, striking a discord—"I don't have that particular problem anymore. There's nothing to interfere with tennis. Of course, I can't *play* tennis, but that's no big deal."

"Kevin." Wren put her hand over his on the keys.

"Yeah. Stop acting like an ass, right?"

"Stop hurting yourself," Wren said gently.

"Hurting myself? You call this hurting myself. Attempting suicide, that was hurting. Doing whatever it is Dad's doing up there, that's hurting. But I'm talking, Wren. I'm keeping the doors of communication open. I'm expressing myself to you."

"Sam's coming in a few minutes. We're going to the

nursery to get his folks a hanging basket for their anniversary. Come with us."

"Nope."

"I wish you would."

"I wish you'd get mad, Wren. I wish you'd say to hell with this piano and with Mom and Dad, with everything."

"It's Dad, then?"

"When I came by his door, I think he was listening to you play. I didn't say anything to him, but he looked a little more alert somehow, like he could be listening. But he probably wasn't."

"Maybe he was. Maybe if you went in and talked to him, he'd hear you."

"No way." Kevin got up and swung the tennis racket above her head, a quick swoop that edged her hair. "I hear Sam," he said, going for the door. "See you later."

He went out the back, leaving Sam and Wren alone in the living room.

"Getting into the hymnbook," Sam said, nodding at the music on the stand.

"You needn't look like the cat who ate the canary," Wren said, dropping the book on the bench.

He looked so smug to her, as if he thought he'd won something. Won her, maybe. Then why did she feel so estranged, so unwieldy and doomed, like a top that was rumbling out its last slow spin before the inevitable tumble?

"I don't just play classical stuff, Sam. Sometimes I actually entertain myself playing show tunes, Paul Simon, things like that. Sometimes I even get out the hymnal. I'm not exactly a freak."

"I've never thought you were," Sam started.

"Then why do you want me to be different from the way I am? You want to take over my life, make me fit into your plans. I can feel it, Sam."

"I don't, Wren. I just want—I don't know what I want. I came in here wanting to go downtown with you. No big deal. Just a walk downtown, but maybe that's not enough for you." He looked helpless, like a misplaced person faced with signs he couldn't read. He wiped his sweaty hands on his jeans and then dug them into his pockets. He felt uncomfortable in this perfect living room with this perfect girl. He didn't belong here. "I'm going," he said. "Are you coming or not?"

"Do you want me to?" Wren turned away from him, spite falling away to dread that he didn't care anymore. She could lose him this fast.

"Of course, I want you to."

"Even when I act like an idiot?"

"I'm a tolerant person." He was grinning. "Bad day, huh?"

"Yeah." She couldn't help but turn to him with a smile of her own. "Don't you ever have them?"

"Mama don't allow it." He put his arms out to her.

"That's where you've got a distinct advantage," Wren said.

"That's the only advantage I've got." Sam took his time holding her.

Kevin opened the blinds in his father's room. Sunlight studded the furniture, brought the corners out of shadow to fix the dimensions of his concealed life.

"Dad," he said softly, putting his hand on the bedpost,

only inches away from his father's head. "Dad, it's lunch time. I brought you something."

Tom didn't move. He was curled under the sheet, knees drawn up, thin back curved away from the light.

"Dad, it's lunchtime. I brought you something to eat," Kevin said again. "I want you to get into the chair. I'll help you."

Still no movement, just a slight moan through motionless lips.

"Dad." He reached out to touch the head, hair stiff and flattened on the sides as if he'd been under the scissors of a demented barber. Kevin brushed the hair down, smoothing it over and feeling the shape of the head under his hand. Why must there be madness there? he wondered. Why is there such loneliness, such fear, when so many people love him?

"Dad, I want you to eat," he said quietly. "I'm going to pick you up and put you in the chair. Then I'm going to feed you, and you are going to eat. Do you hear?" He slid his hand down the neck to the shoulder and pulled.

He had expected resistance, but Tom turned easily under his grip. Lying flat on his back, he stared at the ceiling, although there seemed to be little focus, just a vacant, drooping gaze. "I can't," he mumbled.

"I'll help you." Kevin pushed one arm under Tom's shoulder and with the other hand pulled his knees together, lifting him into his arms. He could feel the stretching of his wrist, flesh pulling away from bone. It hurt, but he backed away from the bed anyway, moving slowly toward the chair.

"I'm going to sit you down now, Dad. Easy does it."

The body sank into the chair, head slumped, arms dangling.

"After lunch, I'll get you in the shower. You look terrible, Dad. You ought to care how you look." He stuck a napkin under the sagging chin and lifted a spoon of egg salad to his father's lips. "It's good, Dad. I already had some. Chew a little. Swallow now. You ought to go downstairs to eat. I could carry you. It's better to eat in the kitchen. Who wants to eat in the bedroom? It's like being in the hospital. If you don't eat, you'll have to go back to the hospital, Dad. You know that, don't you? Is that what you want? Is it safe there? Is that what you like about it? Swallow. Here, suck on this straw. It's lemonade, not a mix either. Fresh. Tell me about the hospital, Dad. What do you like about it? People take care of you, right? You don't have to do anything, right? They're all strangers, aren't they? You don't have to care about them. That's it, isn't it? You don't have to care about them. Take this roll in your hand. I'm going to guide it to your mouth, and I want you to bite it. Hold it now. You're not holding it, Dad. Don't eat it then. Who cares? You don't care, so why should we? I mean, we've all got our own problems, don't we? Listen, Dad, you could get well. I know you could. You've got to find a way to care about us. That's what it is—I know you care about us. You used to. You were a good daddy. I remember you. Remember that time I got lost at the beach? It was like I went crazy. Not a single person on that beach looked familiar to me. I kept stumbling around. I probably went past our blanket three or four times before I found it. I was too scared to really look. I mean, I felt alone. But you

were there, Dad. You and Mom and Wren. We're right here
where we've always been. You've just got to see us. Swallow
that."

He wiped the loose lips with the napkin. "Let's get you
in the shower now, before Grandmother gets home. We'll
have you all cleaned up. You need a shave, too. I want you
to stand up—I'll hold you—and walk to the bathroom."

Tom leaned into him without balance or focus, barely
sliding his feet as Kevin towed him along. In the bathroom,
Kevin put a stool in the shower and turned on the water.

Then he slid Tom's pajama top off, unsnapped his pants
and let them drop to the floor. "Step out of them, Dad.
Help me. Now let's get you into the tub. You've got to help
me now."

He lifted the limp body against his own. It was like
holding a sleeping child or an injured one. He felt the slack,
cool flesh under his hands, the weary, angular body resting
at his chest. He felt life in it. He felt memory, a strange,
long-forbidden sense of oneness.

"I will always love you, Daddy," he said, softly releasing
the body under the spray that struck both of them. He
leaned his father against the tiles and balanced him on the
stool. Then he took a sponge and soap to begin the gentle
washing.

Jolene sat across the booth from Wren and Sam in the
drugstore, the hanging basket balanced on the seat next to
her.

"So," she said, banging her cup against the tabletop to
loosen the ice. "Everything's getting back to normal.
Kevin's just fine. I can tell he is "

"Because he invited you to Sam's on the Fourth," Wren added.

"One of his more obvious indications of sanity," Jolene said agreeably. "But he may have to get along without me. I mean, there are other fish in the sea."

"There are?" Sam squeezed Wren's hand under the table.

"For example, you know the Johnsons down the street from us? Well, their grandson came yesterday to spend the rest of the summer. I saw him this morning. He was on the roof, cleaning out the gutters. Shoulders this broad. A real hunk."

"No doubt you joined him on the roof." Wren laughed.

"Hardly, but I'm planning to get a lot of sun this afternoon."

"Jolene, you wouldn't!"

"I would! And I'd better get at it, too. It's almost noon, and I wouldn't want to keep Hercules waiting." She slipped out of the booth. "See you later."

"Let us hear how it goes," Sam said.

"Never fear. I intend to memorize every moment." Jolene sauntered down the aisle, swinging her bag against his hip.

"I wish I could be like that," Wren said. She pulled her hand away from Sam's and pressed cracker crumbs onto her finger to drop them on a napkin.

"Why?" Sam watched her methodical tidying.

"She's going to have a fine life. She's going to be happy because it's not going to take too terribly much to make her that way."

"You probably worry about happiness too much," Sam said. "I never even think about it."

"That's because you've always been happy."

"I've had disappointments, Wren. I expect I'll have a lot of them. I wish you didn't think everything is so easy for me. You act like you're the only person who ever suffers any, you and Kevin." Sam's voice tightened.

"That's not true."

"But you act that way, like you're the only person in the world who's serious about anything. The truth is, I think you want to win all the time just as much as I do."

"Then don't blame me for it," Wren said.

"Well, don't blame me, either," Sam said, his voice softening a little. "I think we can be all right if we can just trust each other more. I'm not against you, Wren. I'm for you."

"And what about us?"

"I'm for us, too. You ought to know that."

"I'm not sure about anything today."

"Then I'll be sure for both of us," Sam said.

She didn't know how to tell him that that was not enough.

Kevin and Wren went to the lake on a day that turned out to be perfect. A light breeze came down on them through the trees as they walked along the trail to the edge of the water. It was dappled with brilliant sunlight, deep blue and inviting.

"This is where I came with Jack Kensley," Kevin said. "This same spot."

There were people farther down the bank, a family in wet swimsuits grilling burgers, two men fishing in a small boat that looked artificial in the distant stillness.

"It's beautiful. Cold, though." Wren tested the water with her foot.

"And deep. You can keep going down."

"No thanks."

"I wanted to talk anyway," Kevin said. "I guess I wanted to make sure we're still together. I mean, with all the stuff that's happened, everything seems different."

"Does it? I don't feel that. Mother's away. She'll always be away. And Daddy's going back to the hospital. He'll probably be there within a week or two. Of course there's Sam, and I do feel close to him—I guess I love him a lot—but I can't let him change me. I won't, even if he tries. There are so many things I have to decide for myself, Kevin. It's like there are spaces inside, separate places for music and for Sam, for you and our family, for school. But there's another place just for me. Right now I feel as if I have to take special care of that place that's just mine because it's where I can be honest with myself and decide what's right for me no matter what other people want. Is that selfish?"

"So what if it is?"

"Yeah." She grinned. "So what? Let's get wet."

"You first."

"No. You."

"At the same time then," Kevin said.

They slid down the rock, splashing into the water, and came up together.

Chapter 23

There was no big celebration for Wren's birthday, just a quiet dinner in the dining room with Sam and Jolene taking the places left vacant by Karen and Tom. Karen was in Chicago now and Tom was still in his room, the door left slightly ajar so they could listen for him, although he never stirred without their urging or made a sound except in his sleep.

"How much longer?" Jolene asked Bliss in the kitchen while they rinsed the plates between the meal and serving the birthday cake. Only someone like Jolene could ask, someone who knew the inner workings of the family and yet was not attached to it herself. "How much longer can you let him stay?"

"When I can't get him into the bathroom, I'll have to take him back," Bliss said. "That or if he stops eating completely. I keep thinking, hoping that he'll change somehow. If he could just look around and see that Kevin's all right. We're all fine. Maybe then he could come back to us." She closed the dishwasher door and wiped her hands on the dishtowel. "Just listen to me, Jolene. Still hopeful after all this time. You'd think I'd know better."

Chapter Twenty-three

"That's what I like the best about you," Jolene said, lifting down the dessert plates from the cabinet.

Unprepared for a compliment, Bliss busied herself with putting candles on the cake, her back to Jolene. "Fourteen," she said. "Are you in good voice tonight, Jolene? I hope so because I feel a little weepy."

"You carry the cake and I'll take care of the rest," Jolene said, pushing through the swinging door with the plates. *"Ta-dah!"* She stepped aside for Bliss to bring in the lighted cake.

While Jolene led the singing, Bliss, eyes above the candlelight taking them all in, put the cake in front of Wren and then stepped back out of the circle of light to watch their faces. She wanted to make her own wish for her grandchild—all day she had been thinking about it although she was skeptical of wishes. They implied you did nothing but wait, and she knew that a wish had to be worked for. That was what she would wish, then. That Wren would be willing to make her wishes come true.

She watched Wren close her eyes. What did she see in the black space above the white glare of the candles? What kind of vision glowed there? It would be a little wish she made, Bliss knew, because Wren had never asked for big things. She had never expected the extraordinary from other people, just from herself.

"What did you wish for?" Jolene cried as Wren came back to them, leaning her face toward the hot light to blow out the candles.

"She won't tell," Kevin said easily. "Wren never tells."

"That's all you know," Jolene said. "She tells me

241

everything." She glanced around the table at the grinning faces. "Well, practically everything."

After the cake, Bliss and Bill sat on the porch with the door open into the living room where the others had gathered to watch Wren open her gifts. Bliss held Bill's hand in the shadows, hearing the rustle and crack of paper, the sighs and quick spurts of laughter that accompanied Wren's nervous bustle among the ribbons and boxes. It was a good noise in Bliss' house, these sounds of passing years and growing up. She could only wish that Tom heard them, too.

Sam gave Wren a collection of Debussy piano pieces. "I don't know much about classical music, but I'm learning," he said when she had opened the package. "The clerk helped me pick it out. Of course, you can exchange it."

"Play something from it now, Wren," Kevin said.

"I don't want to sight-read, not tonight. Next year I'll play something from it, a present to Sam on my fifteenth birthday." She leaned over to hug him. "Thanks, Sam."

"Well, that's all the loot," Jolene said, tossing through the wrapping paper on the floor. "Now let's do something exciting."

"Like what?" Kevin asked.

"How about a drive-in movie?"

"Jolene, will you never give up?" Wren laughed.

"Not while there's breath in my body."

"No drive-ins," Kevin said. "What I want is to hit some tennis balls."

"*Ag-gag!*" Jolene contorted her body in mock pain.

"Are you playing yet?" Sam asked.

"I've been hitting against the garage for the past few days. Grandmother and I are going out to the courts tomorrow. She wants to make sure I take it easy."

"Then why go tonight?" Jolene was showing her disgust. "After all, this is Wren's birthday, hotshot, not yours. I know what! Let's go up to your room and listen to records."

"Anything to get into my room, huh?" Kevin laughed.

"Exactly."

"Wren and I are going for a walk," Sam said, tossing the loose paper into an empty box. He stood up and took Wren's hand, pulling her up beside him. "Alone."

"This party is disintegrating into nothing." Jolene pouted. "Kevin, why don't you walk me home? We'll walk the long way, past the Johnsons." She grinned. "Don't worry, guys. We'll take the opposite direction from you."

Night was just closing in on the street, and so Wren and Sam watched the lights coming on in the houses, saw jagged translucent shadows solidifying into crisp rectangles of pale yellow. Porch lights glowed their soft, milky light over hedges and spilled into yards where children still played their summer games oblivious of voices urging them in or their own exhaustion.

Wren held Sam's hand lightly, barely touching, until he pulled her fingers tightly against his.

"Wren, do you remember that dinner we had together when your grandparents took us out?"

"Sure."

"You remember you wanted to know what our future would be like, and so I made something up? Well, what I said wasn't exactly made up. It was more what I've always expected to have. I guess it's what a lot of people want—a good life with a decent job, enough money, a family. I was brought up to want those things."

"I want them, too," Wren said. "At least, sometimes I do." She gripped his fingers as if they had only a few more minutes together. Words could separate them now. "But sometimes I can't see room for anything but music because I want to be very good at it, Sam. So I get scared because I don't want to be alone and yet I don't know how I can have everything. It's hard already, making time for everything."

She sighed, feeling his hand tightening in hers. He was holding on.

"Mother told me that she saw two roads—one was exciting and interesting and the other one was ordinary. She chose the exciting one. She chose taking her life in her own hands. I felt so bad toward her then, hearing her tell how she made a choice between a career and me. It hurt so much. But what if I have to make a choice like that? I don't want to. It would be so much better to have everything. I want everything, Sam."

"I know," he said. "I'm beginning to see that, how you can have ambition and still want to be here taking a walk. I can tell you it scared me at first, though, seeing your mother and realizing that you and I aren't the same, not the way I thought we were."

"You gave me Debussy," Wren said.

"Yeah, but I didn't know how to pronounce it."

"So there's something I can teach you. *Deb-yu-see.* Try it."

"There's something else I'd rather try to say." Sam pulled her close to him, one arm around her, the other hand lifting her face to him. "I hope we'll always be together. That was what I wished for tonight when you were making your wish."

"That's the best birthday present you could ever give me," Wren said, and she kissed him right there on Maple Street, while bugs zoomed the street light above their heads and a voice from off a nearby porch sailed across the dark lawn to them, singing softly.

Melanie was on the tennis court, hitting balls with John Weaver. Kevin and Bliss took the court next to them, Kevin facing the sun while Bliss sent him easy serves. His arm was better than his wind, but he knew his breathlessness was partly from nerves, because he couldn't relax with Melanie there.

"You okay, Kevin?" Melanie asked him as he waited for a serve to cross the net.

"Yeah. You?" He moved closer to her, returning the ball.

"I'm glad you're playing again," Melanie said. "I know you've missed it." She leaned against the net post, distracting him.

"Melanie, I've gotta practice now," he said, slamming into the ball.

"Sorry."

She was moving away. He held up his hand to Bliss, who dropped her serve and bounced it into the net.

"Melanie, wait," Kevin called. "I'm sorry." He lumbered toward her awkwardly, as if it were his leg he'd broken. "I guess I've been dreading seeing you, but I've wanted to see you, too. I keep wanting to call you, but I know we said—you said—it was all over."

"I know." She turned slightly away, shielding her face from the sun with her hand. "I didn't know what else to do, Kevin. I just realized I couldn't help you. I mean, I'm not a psychiatrist or anything. I was so scared I'd do or say the wrong thing."

"You could have held my hand. That would have helped." Kevin said bitterly. He didn't want to be angry but just seeing her reminded him of how deserted he'd felt.

"You wanted more than that, Kevin."

"All right, I did." He paused, forcing himself to be calm. She had a right to go her own way. He knew that. She didn't owe him anything, not even this conversation. "I guess I need to know for sure what you want," he said softly.

"I want us to be friends," Melanie said. She reached out to pick a bit of lint off his shirt but let her hand stay there on his sleeve. "After that, we'll have to see how it goes."

"I miss you so much, Mel," he said. He felt tears in his eyes. The sun on the tears made him avert his eyes for a second, then he looked back at her, not caring if she saw.

"I miss you, too. But we have to give it the rest of the summer, Kevin. Give yourself that long to be on your own."

"I'll see you in the fall then," Kevin said, backing away from her hand. He motioned to Bliss to put the ball in play, and when it spun clean and solid over the net at him, he felt his old connection. It felt good.

Karen called. Wren answered, hearing the voice that seemed no more distant than Atlanta. She sat down on the floor in the hall, her back against the wall, and called toward Kevin's door. "It's Mom!"

"Did you have a nice birthday? Tell me what you did," Karen was saying.

Wren watched Kevin coming into the hall. He had stripped down to his tennis shorts and from her perspective on the floor, he seemed so tall, heavier, as if overnight he had grown up.

"Just dinner and a cake," Wren said into the phone. "Sam and Jolene came. Kevin's here, Mother. He's waiting to talk to you." She held out the receiver to him, her face pleading with him to take it.

He clutched the instrument as it dangled from Wren's hand. It was warm already. He pressed it to his ear, hearing the silence and knowing that his own voice would bring hers into his head. He had thought he was ready, expecting as they all had, the inevitableness of her call. He had tried to get ready for this, just as he'd tried to prepare himself to see Melanie, but now he felt defenseless against the gentle battering her voice would give him. He didn't want to hear the distance in it.

"Mother?"

"Kevin, how are you?" The voice was close.

Perhaps that was what he had really dreaded—the illusion of her being on the next block, even in the next room. Her voice was that near.

"I'm fine," he said, pushing out the words on a shallow breath. "I played tennis today, Mother. Not for very long—Grandmother wouldn't let me play long—but it felt okay. It really did. We're playing again tomorrow. I think in another week or so . . ." His voice gave out and so he stopped, waiting for her to respond. He watched Wren, focusing on the simplicity of her face, the calm expression that told him he was doing fine. "Mother, how are you?"

"Working hard," Karen replied. "The job is a twelve-hour one, and I'm trying to do something with this apartment. Some nights I absolutely crawl into bed not caring in the least how it looks, but then the next morning I'm faced with the shambles again and start thinking of what I can do with it. After all, it's where I live."

"Mother, when Wren and I come for Thanksgiving, I want to talk to you."

"What about, Kevin?" He could hear panic in her voice. It rose above her businesslike phone demeanor like a coded message that only he could interpret. She was afraid for him, not for herself. "Are you all right, Kevin? Tell me the truth."

"Don't worry, Mother. Nothing's wrong. I just want to talk to you. You know, really talk." He paused, hoping she'd interfere before he was forced to say more than he was prepared to say. "I just think we have things to talk about."

"So do I, Kevin. I'm glad you want to. I can hardly wait to see you."

"Mother, here's Wren again," Kevin said.

"I love you, Kevin. I want to let you know how to reach me. Can you take down the number?"

"Wren will." Kevin handed the phone back to his sister and slipped into his room. He could hear Wren repeating the digits she had just written in the phone book. He heard the rest of the conversation—Wren's hushed reply to a question about their father's return to the hospital, a more audible response about Bliss and Bill, heard her laugh once recounting how he'd been dunked at the carnival. He heard Wren drawing their mother into their circle, making her there with them, smoothing the ragged edges. She was accepting the distance between them and by doing so, was making it smaller, more traversable. He could do that, too. It was something he could learn.

On Saturday, when Wren came down for breakfast, Kevin was there, his head bent over a bowl of cereal and his eyes on the sports page.

"What's this?" Wren whispered to Bliss, who was forking bacon out of the frying pan.

"Don't know," Bliss said with her eyes. She was dressed, ready to go to the hospital.

"I'll be ready in thirty minutes," Wren said aloud. She put a strip of bacon and a slice of buttered toast on a napkin to take upstairs with her.

When she came down, Kevin was dressed and waiting. "I'm coming, too," he said.

They got into Bliss' Cadillac, Wren in the middle. They all felt stiff, crowded against each other but careful not to touch. It was so hard, this starting out that seemed so strange and unrehearsed, yet so dreadfully familiar.

Bliss turned onto the highway, easing them into the traffic that sped toward what seemed like an endless expanse of open space. Inside they were closed up, silently preparing themselves for their ordeal, building defenses, studding up walls, partitioning interiors against despair. Then Bliss began to hum. It was a soft sound, barely audible over the engine's music, but Wren heard it. The humming fell open to song, and Wren closed her eyes to find the harmony.

Kevin heard then, too. He felt Wren relaxing beside him. Her hands turned soft in her lap, and he put his hand over hers. He wasn't sure he knew the lyric but the tune was familiar, one of his grandmother's old favorites. He doubted he would add much, a ragged note now and then, a jumble of words, but at least he would be with them.

He took a deep breath and croaked out a little noise. It sounded better than he'd expected. And so they went the distance, covering the miles between themselves and Tom, singing as they went.

Sue Ellen Bridgers won immediate recognition with her highly acclaimed first novel, HOME BEFORE DARK. She is the recipient of the Christopher Medal for her second novel, ALL TOGETHER NOW. Both books were published by Knopf.

She lives in Sylva, North Carolina, with her husband, Ben, and their three children.

Grateful acknowledgment is made to April Music, Inc. for permission to reprint lyrics from *You May Be Right* and *Sometimes A Fantasy* by Billy Joel. Both songs Copyright © 1979, 1980 Impulsive Music, Inc. and April Music, Inc. All rights administered by April Music, Inc., 1350 Avenue of the Americas, New York, New York 10019. Used by permission. All rights reserved. International Copyright Secured.